The Sand People

a collection of magical realism
and other stories

by

J A Croome

Cover Design:
Apple Pie Graphics, KZN, South Africa

Cover Image: iStock © ID: 1426661526

eBook Design:
My eBook, Cape Town, South Africa

First Edition: 20 March 2024
ISBN: 978-0-6399831-5-8 (Print Book)
ISBN: 978-0-6399831-6-5 (eBook)

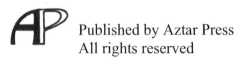

Dedication

Dr. Beric John Croome
23 May 1960 to 22 April 2019

your name is written on my heart

Contents

Page

The Sand People

First came the scout. She peered out of the crack in a rock, then scurried over Bennie's left foot as it lay scorching in the sun. Stunted by years of soaring temperatures and no rain, the camel thorn acacia scarcely provided enough shade to cover him and his all-important travelling trunk. His legs and his feet, in their old leather velskoene that he'd worn for his first Tweede Nuwejaar carnival over ten years ago, stuck out into the heat.

Last new year, and the one before, and before that too, he'd said to Carly, 'When business is better, I'll buy a new pair of shoes for the next parade.' Then Klein Ben came along, the recession hit, and, somehow, new shoes were less important than buying food and keeping the shop stocked.

Unblinking, Bennie watched the ant clamber to the top of his shoe, a mountain. He'd driven out of Droerivier near the Namibian border at sunrise when the morning was still cool, and he was still energised by the sale of a few items. He should have stayed by the car when the sand had swamped the carburettor. But, despite not seeing another soul for hours, he'd abandoned it. As he started walking, he dragged the suitcase from the back seat, the R200 notes from his sales crunching with a satisfying crackle in his pocket, convinced another car would come along and lift him to the next village.

By midday, he'd also abandoned his walk, forced by the heat to seek shelter under this skeletal tree and wait. The hours passed in silence so great that, as the scout ant paused, her antennae probing this way and that way, he could hear her mandibles crunching with excitement. He sat unmoving, only wiping away the sweat gathering on his forehead and running rivulets down the red dust on his cheeks once she'd scurried down onto the ground, disappearing into the rocks and sand behind him.

The shadow of the tree grew longer and thinner. Later, Bennie's fears of becoming a dried-up husk of skin and bone grew fat with his aloneness, and he knew both God and humanity had abandoned him. Soon, the anonymous wind would scatter the ashes of his dust into the vast desert sands. Through his despair, Bennie heard a scratching buzz.

She was back.

With thousands of her nestmates, the scout ant marched her procession up and over his foot, over the faded road and into the rocks from which she'd first appeared with a determination driven by hunger and the smell of a successful hunt.

In the dehydrated confusion of his memory, Bennie remembered his grandfather saying, 'Stay away from the black ants, Jong Bennie; when they're hungry, they eat a whole village! Ek's nie geroek nie, Bennie, when I say they'll destroy it in an hour — munch, munch, munch!'

Then he heard his grandfather whisper that where the Matabele ants marched, there must be a village.

If he stayed, the heat would kill him.

If he left his travel trunk behind and lived, starvation would kill him, for his last merchandise was packed into its shabby leather. After the grinding recession of the previous eighteen months, the money from his few sales in Droerivier was not enough to save him.

'When will you be back, Papa?' Klein Ben had asked.

'Soon,' he'd promised, packing the last of his stock into his trunk. 'Where I'm going, people haven't seen such good stock in years.'

'If you don't sell everything, we can't go on with the shop,' Carly said, wringing her hands with their nails broken and skin chapped from too many hours spent cleaning someone else's house for extra money to send Klein Ben to a good school.

'I know,' he'd said, then kissed them both goodbye.

How will they survive if the desert sucks the life out of me? He watched the column of ants in their vigorous trek towards salvation. With the stones packed hard into the dirt, the road had defeated his old car but was barely an obstacle to the marching ants.

Pushing himself to his feet, he hooked his hand into the trunk strap, swinging it onto his shoulders. Gripping the three-quarters-full case more firmly, he settled the heavy weight across his shoulders, staggering after the ants, following them to the source of their food: the village he was convinced lay just over the horizon, waiting at the end of the path like a pot of gold at the end of a multi-coloured rainbow.

Bennie staggered to a halt when the sun was turning from fiery gold to soft pink, and the first hint of the night's coolness touched his burning, blistered lips. The ants disappeared into a giant termite mound over the last rolling sand dune on the horizon. He swore he could hear the screams of the dying termites, crushed to death by the cruel pincers of the more powerful Matabele ants, but it was his own screams he heard, for there — where the dune dipped into the valley of sand — lay the remains of the village the ants had already devoured.

A few ramshackle tin huts; a broken sign, swaying in the gusts of wind, clanking against a steel pole, said "Welcome to Steendorp, the hottest town on earth"; beneath that was a faded advertisement for Kojo Tea, taunting Bennie with the sight of a painted cup, steam rising and the promise of "the best cup of Ceylon Tea you'll ever drink!"; scattered between the huts, dozens of strange metal chimneys poked out the ground, their metal flues clanging and whirring in the rising night wind: all that was left of the village that would have saved him, both body and soul.

With a heavy thud, Bennie dropped his case, the contents spewing out onto the desiccated rocks, some so dry they crumbled under the featherweight of ladies' lingerie in all shades from sexy black to a pretty pale pink. He fell to his knees, uncaring that he crushed a man's watch, still in its plastic box, into the ground, sobbing in great dry heaves, for there wasn't enough water left in his body for real tears, just as there wasn't a drop of hope left in his soul.

The new politicians had promised a new life, a better life for all, but — while they sat in their mansions with fire pools and home cinemas — Bennie was alone and dying in this desert where once his ancestors had roamed free. While they had thrived on its bounty, he and Carly and Klein Ben lived trapped in a tin shack in the Cape Flats.

He had tried to do something, to change something, by coming to this godforsaken desert that had once been home to his people. He had ignored the others who said it was too risky, too hard, too dangerous a road to take.

Now the desert was a beast, sucking the life out of him like the marauding Matabele ants were sucking the life out the termites, marching back the way they'd come with two-three-four dead termite bodies clasped in their jaws, marching right past his nose as he smelt the dust and the dirt and the death of hope creeping up his nostrils.

He lay there as the last of the day's heat burnt itself into a delicate night dew, and a multitude of shadows and bobbing lights arose from the sand surrounding him. Gentle hands rolled him over, moistening his lips and washing his face, as soft voices whispered in an ancient language, a language he'd heard from his father's father's lips, but one he'd never spoken, for life was different today.

Today, there was no time for the old rituals and the old ways; there was barely time in each day to kiss your son good morning and your wife goodbye as you rushed out to the shop, trying to make a living, before trudging home with nothing to show after you'd paid the taxi fares and bought the milk for Klein Ben's porridge ... but here, as the sand shadows encircled him, speaking in the voices of his grandmothers and his grandfathers, in the voices of the ancient gods whispering that hope is never dead; hope is the flicker of a fading star in the desert sky and it takes only one — one! — of the sand people to carry that light from generation to generation and lead the way into the future. In his generation, they said, Bennie was the one chosen to carry the light.

But Bennie could no longer believe in dreams of light and of hope. With a sigh, he sank into the darkness, the voices fading even as the shadows picked him up, gathering his suitcase and the merchandise scattered in the desert rocks, carrying him to a luminous white door dug into the rocks covered by the rolling desert dunes ...

Bennie thought he'd died but couldn't figure out if he was in heaven or hell because he'd always thought hell was hot and heaven gleamed with light. But the cool room he woke in was dimly lit with a soft yellow glow from a single lamp on the table next to his bed. The woven grass lampshade cast dashes of light on the walls, almost like a 70's disco ball, but without the revolving silver flashes.

He sat up, throwing off the thin sheet covering him as he swung his feet to the floor, and saw that the walls were carved from rough red rock, the colour of the deepest desert sands. The floor, cool under his bare feet, was carved from the same material.

The walls were gaily decorated — a proud gemsbok, its regal stare frozen through a camera lens onto glossy photo paper, mounted in a gold plastic frame; a tapestry, its faded pink and white roses interwoven with green stitches, asking "What is a house without a Father?"; and a curtain rod from which two drawn white curtains hung haphazardly, splashed with the rock art of his ancient people in shades of rust and ochre.

Bennie staggered across to the curtains, flinging them open, only to recoil in shock as he stared at another red rock wall. He stumbled back, his lungs gasping, surprisingly fresh air flowing in from a vast round tube leading up through the ceiling of rock where, at the distant end, he could just make out the flapping metal flues blowing in the desert wind.

He rubbed the palms of his hands into his eyes to clear them, then slowly took stock of his surroundings. His traveller's trunk lay open on an old three-seater bench, carved with intricate blackwood spindles and strung with riempie thongs sturdy enough to hold the weight of the case with barely a dimple. Riffling through it, Bennie saw that all his goods, even the crushed watch, were cleaned and neatly packed.

Except for the cheap, six-for-less-than-R100 underpants he wore, his clothes, too, were washed and folded neatly next to an old enamel wash basin and pitcher, blue with red trim and, on the handle, the first scatterings of rust growing like mould. Pure and clean, the water in the pitcher splashed cold on his skin as he poured it from the jug into the basin and washed the sense of unreality from his mind.

Dressed, Bennie was covered with ambiguous confidence: in clean clothes, his velskoene free of dust, the crisp sound of R200 notes still crackling in his pocket, he felt he could make a few good sales again. The thought of just who his potential customers might be beyond this strange cave room tempered that confidence with uncertainty and a little fear.

Opening the door, he saw his room led into a long passage dotted with numbered doors, an underground hotel corridor, at the end of which was a flight of carved stairs. Light and music, the sound of laughter and clinking glasses tumbled towards him. Several passages, each with a sign, spread out from the landing above the stairs: "Bathroom", "Dining Room", "Gift Shop/Exit", and "The Sand Shelter."

The noise mainly came from the latter, and bracing himself, Bennie started climbing. As he pushed the double-hinged door and stepped over the threshold, an old Abdullah Ibrahim song embraced him, curling its haunting melody around the hum of the crowd propping up the bar, mingling with the smell of beer, brandewyn and sweat. The barman, a pale-faced man with long black hair spilling over his shoulders and a short-cropped beard with a sprinkling of grey, was the first to notice him.

'How'zit, bru!' he called cheerfully. 'You've finally joined the land of the living again, have yah?' He slapped a brandy and ginger ale on the counter before Bennie, ice cubes rattling against the glass. 'First one's on the house; after that, yah pay, just like the rest.'

'You're a thief, Jake!'

'Ask for a discount!'

'Don't pay these prices, stranger!'

Smiling warily at the raucous hoots, Bennie made his way through the people milling around. People just like anywhere, in any bar, in any town. Some played pool at a dimly lit table to the left of the bar; the clack of cues hitting the ball punctuated the beat of Ibrahim's Song for Sathima. A few couples swayed together on a tiny dancefloor; men and women jostled for orders and space at the bar counter. With each step, with each 'hi' and 'howzit', Bennie's uncertainty and fear left him. By the end of his first sip, he was scanning the crowd for potential customers.

When he met the gaze of a young woman, almost as pretty as Carly had been when he first met her, she smiled, raising her beer, and asked, 'Hey, Mister, where's your trunk?'

That was all Bennie needed. For the next hour, he was in heaven: every salesman's heaven, for the friendly strangers crowded around Bennie and his trunk and bought every last item he had left. Even the crushed watch was sold: a toothless old man, berry eyes gleaming in a wrinkled face, cackled with glee as he began de-constructing the broken watch Bennie had sold him for R10.

The following day, waiting for the lift the underground hotel had organised for him, he shook hands with Jake.

'Thanks for saving me,' Bennie said, wanting to say more, settling for a firm handshake instead. 'Not once, but twice.'

'Go easy on the brandewyn next time, bru!' The bartender laughed and clapped him on the shoulder.

'I'd have been dead if you hadn't heard me shouting. And your customers bought all my stock. I haven't had such good sales in years.'

'We don't get many travelling salesmen in Steendorp. We're hard to find in all this desert.' Jake squinted at the airshafts dotting the landscape, then bent to pick off a small black ant marching across his shoe. 'But we didn't hear you shouting. Down below, when we're in the rock rooms, everything is soundproof.' He carefully dropped the ant into the shade of the signpost advertising Kojo Tea. 'You saved yourself, bru, walking in large as life, with your trunk on your shoulder and a smile on your face, asking for the best room in the hotel!'

In the heat of that new day, under the same burning sun that had nearly sucked the life out of him, ice ran into Bennie's veins, chilling his skin with goosebumps as his heart thudded in his chest. For a second, he felt dizzy, hearing the murmur of long-dead voices, hearing the cry of the sand people still living in the desert, but it was only the sound of a truck's engine getting closer and closer.

'Stay well,' he said to Jake, climbing into the tow truck and, with a last wave to Jake and a few of the townspeople who popped out of their doors into the heat to say goodbye, Bennie pointed the driver toward his broken-down car.

Years later, when Klein Ben — now a doctor of medicine at an upmarket private hospital in Tshwane — brought the grandchildren to stay with Bennie and Carly, Bennie would take the little ones into the desert of their ancestors for a night.

There, under the star-studded midnight sky, time was slow again, and life was sweet, still filled with promise and hope and dreams... he'd build a fire to ward off the night chill and, as they braaied marshmallows on the fire and drank hot tea made with condensed milk, he'd gather his grandchildren around his feet.

He'd tell them how one day he'd followed a column of marching Matabele ants to the village that always lived beneath the hot, dry rocks of the vast wilderness. He'd tell them how his life had been twice saved and how, on his return from the desert, filled once more with hope, he had slowly changed his life for the better.

Then he'd whisper into their hearts tales of the sand people, that line of souls stretching both backwards and forwards in time: the living link between his past and their future, embracing all that was, all that is and all that is yet to come for Bennie, for his children's children and for the dusty land in which generations of their family live and die.

The Seventh Silence

I am beautiful.
I am implacable.
And I am terrible.
Throughout the ages, people have feared me.
Even in this modern world, where technology
masquerades as magic and reason rules superstition,
they shudder when they talk of me. Some call me La
Meurte; others, The Grim Reaper. Most whisper only
my true name: Death.

Lost in their fear, no one sees the grace in my
eternal silence. Except, perhaps, the descendants of
the ancient !XoiSan people. They seek me in the dry
winds of the Kalahari Desert; they find me in the
spirit of the sacred eland they hunt, and they come to
me through the painted faces adorning the walls of
their derelict tin shacks crowding the edges of the
great northern city of e'Goli ...

MacKenzie Carter was coming home to die.
Oh, he called it home, but he'd never set foot in South
Africa before. He looked down at this foreign land as
the South African Airways Flight SA204 from New
York circled high over Tshwane, then arced south to
head over a vast sea of shacks. The shantytown, a
creeping tsunami, threatened to overwhelm the
glittering skyscrapers of nearby Johannesburg. Mac
wondered if those rickety tin shacks were filled with
strangers, each as broken as he, each flocking to meet
their dreams — or their doom — in a hostile city far
from the place of their birth.

The aircraft tyres thumped onto the runway.
Mac, clenching his jaw against the shards of pain
stabbing his gut, wondered why he'd answered the
call of this stark and strange land: a country, his father

had once told him, that lived in bold colours and loud noises, cradling the most profound mysteries in her soul even as the secrets of a dark past shaded her heart.

Mac stepped onto the aeroplane stairs, minimising his pain with a slow descent to the tarmac. Grateful for the silver-and-orange bus waiting to take the disembarking passengers to the distant airport terminal, he breathed deeply. This air carried magic in its scent, tingling along his nerves and filling his heart with more life than he'd felt in the last month. The bright, golden sunshine warmed him, chasing away the ever-present cold permeating his body since he'd received the diagnosis.

'They call me the bad news doc,' the oncologist had said, almost apologetically.

Mac's heart had thumped erratically in his chest, his forehead and hands suddenly dripping sweat. He'd put off going for his annual health check-up — he was always too busy, too tired, too scared. Whatever excuse he'd used, he'd delayed the doctor's visit until the pain had forced him to see his GP.

'How bad?' he'd asked, proud that his voice remained steady despite the dryness of his mouth, an outward calm defying the terror skittering through him.

'The tumour's inoperable, and the cancer is aggressive.' The doctor had shrugged, detached from this little human drama, distanced from Mac by the scientific results on his desk. 'With intensive chemotherapy, you may survive six months, possibly a year.'

Chemotherapy … Mac had watched his wife die of cancer, years of chemo treatment destroying her quality of life with side effects and sickness.

'How long without treatment?'

'Maybe six to eight weeks.' Pushing his black-framed glasses back up his nose, the oncologist's remote gaze flickered briefly in Mac's direction before retreating to the safety of his lab reports.

Mac had thanked him and left, driving straight to the nearest travel agency to book his flight home.

Here he stood, the first Carter to set foot in South Africa since his South African father, a !XoiSan human rights lawyer, had fled the apartheid government to follow his blonde, blue-eyed and pregnant American lover to her home in McComb, Mississippi.

They were both dead these past forty years, killed by a bomb blast in the Temple Hill Missionary Baptist Church. Their work for the American Civil Rights movement had annoyed the wrong people, and, at ten years old, Mac became an orphan.

He knew it was his imagination, but as he collected his luggage from the fast-moving carousel and walked through the automatic doors into the international arrivals hall with careful, hesitant steps so unlike his old confident stride, he heard an echo of his father's voice saying, 'Welcome home, son, welcome to the land of your ancestors.'

'TAXI! Taxi for Mr Car-tee-ay! Taxi!'

Lost in the emotion binding his heart tight in his chest, Mac almost missed the mangled pronunciation of his name.

He swung around and saw a slender, wizened man waving a placard. The man — about seventy years old, Mac thought from the wrinkles in his yellowish-brown skin — wore blue jeans, a white shirt frayed at the tips of the collar, and a brown tie with a beige-and-red geometric pattern. His peaked hat was made of pale antelope skin; the band of the hat matched a bracelet he wore, both some kind of animal fur, plaited and threaded with brightly coloured glass beads. The placard declared "FIRE FINISHER SHUTTLE SERVICES – South African

Airways Flight SA204 from New York – Mr MacKenzie David Carter."

Mac had booked online with another service. 'Where's the driver from Sun Shuttle Service?'

'Don't worry, Mister, don't worry! We are the same service, just with a new name,' the man said. 'I am still the best driver in e'Goli!' He smiled, a broad, gap-toothed grin, as he gently pried Mac's fingers loose from the heavy suitcase. Mac gratefully released the suitcase into his eager grasp, feeling guilty, for the driver, eyes as old as the land and a tiny, wiry body, looked too frail to lift the heavy weight.

But looks were deceptive — these days, when Mac looked in the mirror, he was leaner and meaner than ever before as the illness took its toll on the extra weight he'd carried for years — and the driver easily hefted Mac's case as he said, 'Did you have a good journey, Mr Car-tee-ay?'

Tiredness, uncertainty and a sudden shaft of pain made Mac snarl, 'My name's Carter, not Car-tee-ay! And who are *you*?'

'I am me!' The driver pointed at his name printed in bold black on a gold badge decorated with the image of a burning campfire and introduced himself with a complicated twist of strange clicks. 'I am !XuRama, son of the First People. Just like you, Mr Car-tee-ay,' he said, with a grin that hinted at mischief and mystery. 'You, too, have the blood of the First People in your veins, *né*?'

Not waiting for an answer, he laughed. 'You can't say my name, so you can call me Rama. Living in America, you have lost the speech of your ancestors.' He clicked his tongue again — to Mac, a sorrowful sound — then laid a guiding hand on Mac's lower back, exactly where the centre of Mac's pain coiled and writhed.

'*Tsí! Tsí!* Come! Come!' Rama said as Mac's pain eased into a dull twinge. 'We must hurry, or we'll be trapped in the M24 home-time traffic to the city.'

The waiting shuttle cab was unexpected — an old two-tone VW Combi covered with strange, primitive decorations; the bottom half painted a verdant green. Across the top half, almost as if running across wild grassy plains far from the city, huntsmen carrying spears chased a herd of brown antelope. In another fresco, disappearing over the roof of the van, other animals — a smaller antelope, a snake, a lion, and a strange flying porcupine with sparks of fire shooting from its quills — leapt, slithered, or ran.

The hunters held Mac's attention. In some buried attic of his mind, he heard his father's voice telling him tales of the great hunts of the Kalahari before the black people had come from the northern hills and the white people had come from the sea, both squeezing the First People's ancestors further and further into the great sand face of the Kalahari.

Fascinated by the figures, Mac traced his finger along sticklike legs and flimsy spears. His blood began to bubble, for the more he looked at them, the more the figures danced with a living energy. The faint echo of voices, shouting in triumph as a young hunter threw his spear, the sound of that strange clicking language shimmering in the air, made Mac dizzy until he realised that, with a strength belying his small stature, Rama had swung the suitcase into the back of the van so hard the old car shuddered on its springs and the huntsmen were, after all, nothing but painted figures on an old VW van.

'Where are you staying, Mr Car-tee-ay?'

'The Michaelangelo Towers in Sandton,' he said. A little bereft since that gentle touch had lifted from his back, a little shaken by the impact of the painted figures, Mac didn't bother correcting the mangling of his name this time.

Rama forced the car into gear, and the van
chugged out of the parking onto the busy M24 route.
Merrily unaware of the annoyed hooting of other cars
speeding past, Rama kept Mac entertained with
unbroken conversation.

'When I was a young *!'hoă* — a very young
man — I lived in the Kalahari Desert, far from this
beast of a city,' he said, 'I'd sit around campfires with
our people, the children of the First People, and listen
to the elders tell the stories of our past. My
grandfather would tell of the time he felt the seventh
silence come from the sky god.

'That day, my grandfather was a young man.
His father's father lay fighting |Gaunab, the evil one.

'As we had grown fat and heavy from eating
the gifts of the sacred eland,' he said, tapping the
sidebar of the window where the head and horns of a
large painted antelope crept into the van, '|Gaunab,
living inside the old man until he screamed with the
pain every time he moved, grew fat and heavy from
my ancestor's spirit.

'Too young to join the hunt, my grandfather
was alone, not knowing what to do, where to turn,
until |Kaggen, disguised in his favourite body of the
sacred eland, came out of the heat mist rising from the
sands. As he grazed closer and closer, my grandfather
crept back into the hut, staying silent, watching over
his father's father as he lay dying, until |Kaggen
called to him through the door.

'"Do not be afraid. Do not be afraid of the vast
silence." |Kaggen said. "We all must walk the lands of
dust until the seventh silence comes, and then we
leave, our footsteps blown away on the wind, carried
into the hearts of our children and our children's
children."'

Rama fell silent, distracted by the need to coax
the old van into continued life on the busy highway

until Mac couldn't stand the eerie quiet. 'What happened?' he asked.

'My grandfather watched as |Kaggen came right into the hut. With his great horns as gentle as a mother's arms, he lifted my grandfather's father's father onto his back. Then he walked outside again, taking the old man further and further into the heat mist until they disappeared into the seventh silence.'

Small brown eyes met Mac's in the review mirror. Filled with wisdom and compassion and knowledge so primaeval, the tears Mac had been unable to cry since hearing his diagnosis rose from his heart into his throat, clamouring to be released in a howl of despair. He fell into that gaze, somehow gaining enough strength and momentary relief from the pain to ask, 'Did he ever come back from the silence?'

He thought he knew what the seventh silence was, but he was afraid to ask, afraid to mention the word 'death' because it made the reason for his journey to this country too real, too near.

'He was older than the flood that cleansed the world, and his time had come to return with |Kaggen into the final silence,' Rama said, shifting gears with a horrible grating sound that had Mac grabbing the dilapidated plastic strap hanging from the van's ceiling. 'Most never return from the eland's journey to the seventh silence, but some strong spirits, a few chosen ones, are sent back to the here-world to complete their undone tasks.'

Mac had never believed in newspaper reports that spoke of near-death experiences and people returning from the dead, so after a polite 'Lucky them,' he leaned back to stare at the passing scenery as the VW lumbered on.

Two enormous water-cooling towers loomed along the horizon. Clearly abandoned, they were, like the van, painted with scenes of elongated human and animal figures in shades of red, white, brown and black.

One tower was dominated by a colossal human figure with the head of a bird, zigzag legs and large, outstretched hands, dancing in front of a campfire, surrounded by diminutive figures of men and women, their painted hands clapping a silent rhythm. Beyond the campfire, clusters of scenes from another world climbed the walls of the towers: a fantastic elephant surrounded by tiny stick figures carrying spears, bees — or perhaps flies — swarmed around the beast's trunk. A feline with exaggerated teeth and claws prowled through the painted grass. On the other tower, a giant antelope with majestic horns — an eland, Mac thought Rama had called the similar image on the van — fled sticklike huntsmen armed with bows and arrows.

Strung between the towers was a bridge, and as Mac watched, the small figure of a man climbed onto the parapet. Holding his arms wide, without the slightest pause, the figure fell forward, nose-diving straight into the abyss below. Before Mac could do more than gasp, he saw the thick cord spiral through the air, joining the man's feet to the parapet.

'Bungee jumping,' Rama said. 'Crazy people.'

Mac laughed. Crazy, alright, for as the man had soared through the air before he'd noticed the bungee cord, Mac could have sworn he saw the painted head and horns of the majestic eland dominating the east tower's wall slowly bend and sway as if to catch the man as he fell.

'Death comes soon enough. We shouldn't tempt the gods to take us from our children too early,' Rama said. 'Do you have children waiting for you in America, Mr Car-tee-ay? A son who will mourn you when you die one day?'

'I'm widowed,' Mac said curtly, 'My wife died before we had children.'

'*Ai! Ai! Ai!*' Rama crooned, shaking his head in sympathy, and said not another word until he dropped Mac off at the imposing portal of the five-star hotel in the middle of the busy northern suburb.

'This is not where the city lives, Mr Car-tee-ay,' he said, helping Mac out of the van. 'I can show you where e'Goli breathes with life, real life.'

Life. Mac had too little of that left and not enough to do to fill what little there was.

'Pick me up at 08h00 tomorrow,' he instructed. Was the strange light that turned Rama's eyes from brown to gold his imagination or due to the R200 tip he'd slipped into the driver's eager palm?

The next day, when Mac emerged into the overpowering heat of the morning, the painted van was waiting. Rama, his wiry body springing up and down with barely suppressed excitement, greeted him.

'Quick, quick, Mr Car-tee-ay,' he said. 'We have much to do and much to see! Today, you'll visit the city few tourists ever see.' As the van door stuck, he banged it open and hustled Mac inside, patting his shoulder as he chortled, 'But you're not the usual tourist, are you?' He scuttled round to the driver's seat and hopped in, throwing Mac that impish look again as if only they shared a delicious secret.

'What do you mean?'

'Anyone looking at you can see that you carry within you the blood of the !Xoi San. You and I, the First People, can go places others can't.'

Mac, grouchy after another restless night filled with vague dreams and sharp pain, already regretted agreeing to tour the underbelly of Johannesburg. All he wanted was to spend the day retracing the steps of his parents, visiting the old John Vorster Square, where his father had been detained and charged with treason for his love affair with a white American woman; he wanted to sit on the edge of Zoo Lake, where his parents first met at an anti-apartheid protest march, and he wanted to soak up the heat of the African sun in mindless contemplation of how his future had shrunk from decades to weeks.

'Make it a quick tour, Rama,' he said, reaching up to touch one of the painted huntsmen adorning the VW's ceiling. He'd not noticed it yesterday, there on the domed roof, stalking across the painted landscape, separated from his tribe by a window and a hanging plastic strap. 'Tsssjh!' Mac exclaimed, pulling his hand back from the tip of the painted spear his finger had just traced. A pinprick of blood oozed from Mac's finger; staring in disbelief at the figure, his heart rate slowed down again when he noticed the tip of a broken piece of metal piercing the worn plastic covering the roof.

'Here, in the land of your ancestors, you must be careful where you touch, Mr Car-tee-ay,' Rama advised with a solemn nod, 'for in beauty lies hidden pain; in pain, hidden freedom.'

Mac laid his head back on the seat, a rip in the hard red plastic jabbing his neck above the collar of his shirt. He ignored Rama, ignored the pain, the heat, simply closing his eyes against the tide of nausea and fear threatening to drown him in its intensity.

'Mac! Mac!' His father's voice woke him, but he knew he was dreaming. His father had died instantly in that letter bomb, even as his mother had lingered for five days before dying. Now, here in the land where he'd been conceived in a forbidden and dangerous love, Mac was nearing his time of dying, too.

'Mac! Wake up!' Hearing his father's voice again, he wondered if he wasn't already dead, slipping away from the pain mangling his gut and the regrets clawing his heart, slipping away in the back seat of an old 60's VW hippie bus.

When he dragged his eyelids open, he wasn't dead, and it wasn't his father calling him.

Rama's face, split with that gap-toothed grin, fast becoming as irritating to Mac as it was endearing, hovered over him.

'*Kom*, Mr Car-tee-ay,' he said, 'come with me. We are in the heart of e'Goli.'

The smell hit Mac first: raw sewerage, rotting vegetables and the decaying body of an old brown-and-white dog. He had no time to gag a protest, for Rama hurried him out the van, shouting greetings in the strange clicks and clucks of his language to the people teeming along the narrow lane between hastily erected shacks. Labels and signs that Mac recognised from billboards back in the States covered the walls of some shacks; the now familiar shapes and colours of wild animals and stick hunters decorated the walls of others.

Dizzy from the dream and the overpowering heat, smells and sounds, Mac cried out to Rama to stop, for the walls of the shack city were closing in on him, the painted faces swarming off the walls, painted mouths twisting into cavernous smiles, painted hands floating through the air to pluck and pinch at his clothes, his hair, his arms. Hollow, disembodied sounds thundered through his head in a cacophony of clicks and calls: the cry of a prehistoric huntsman, the roar of a desert lion and the frantic gallop of a dying eland.

He stumbled, gasping Rama's name, sweat pouring off him, running in tiny rivulets down the corrugations in the shack wall against which he fell.

'Rest, Mac, rest.' He knew that Rama spoke, not the ghost of his father, but it was Rama transformed, standing in the painted doorway of a shack on the other side of the dirt lane when he opened his eyes.

Wearing only a rough loincloth made of animal skin, Rama held a long wooden hand-bow with its quiver of arrows slung over his shoulder. Strips of hard-shelled seeds, tied around his wrists and ankles, rattled with a soft susurration as he waved Mac inside.

Mac, more lost and out of his depth than he'd been since his diagnosis, simply stepped over the threshold. The canvas flap Rama held up fell back into place with the whoosh of an owl's wings, closing Mac into a darkness flickering with rays of light streaming through minuscule gaps where ramshackle joins barely held the corrugated iron walls together.

Surrounded by a silence so deep it muted the noise of the busy township beyond the small shack, Mac's sight gradually adjusted to the dimness. Rama sat on a wooden box marked "Panda Paraffin Stoves." Hunched over a lit stove, the red enamel burnt black in places and the open flames curling blue with heat, he stirred an aromatic brew in a dented aluminium kettle.

The same primitive drawings Mac had seen everywhere covered the shack's inner walls; here, red lines fringed with white dots disappeared into the light-filled fissures in the shack walls, like paths disappearing into the blinding heat of the rising sun.

'Sit, Mr Car-tee-ay, sit here next to the fire to warm,' Rama invited, pointing to a sandy hollow on the edge of the circle of light cast by the flames from the paraffin cooker. As hot as it was in the shack, with the heat of the stove and the temperature soaring as morning became midday, Mac realised he was shivering and cold and so weary his bones ached.

Taking an empty cup — enamelled in pale green and covered with the inevitable painted scenes — Rama poured the steaming liquid into the mug, an enticing smell of blackcurrants wafting in Mac's direction.

'Drink some buchu,' Rama said, 'it'll give you strength and wisdom, a gift from your ancestors.'

Mac's hesitation in reaching for the mug didn't escape Rama. 'Have faith, Mac,' he whispered, once again sounding too much like Mac's memory of his father.

'Oh, what the hell!' Mac said and took the mug. He was dying anyway, and whatever was in that tin cup could only kill him quicker. He gagged at the first spicy taste, but by his third sip, he drifted into a cloud of calm, aware of Rama watching him closely. Had he been drugged? Would his mutilated body be discarded in one of the vast piles of garbage outside?

There was no one left, back in America, who would care enough to report him missing. Perhaps one or two of his work colleagues. They'd tried to dissuade him from coming here, quoting the high murder rate in South Africa, the threat of lions in the street and the risk of women with AIDS waiting to entrap an unwary tourist.

As the warmth of buchu seeped into his veins and Rama started to chant in a high-pitched rhythmic tone, Mac slumped back against the nearest wall and gulped down the rest of the tea.

Minutes or aeons later, he heard a growl. Opening his eyes, he saw a lion sitting on the box marked "Panda Paraffin Stoves," its golden mane framing a face that held a shadow of Rama, the fierce animal eyes containing a hint of mischievousness.

Behind the magnificent creature, surrounding them both in a tight circle, stood a host of sticklike people, ephemeral slivers of shadows, chanting and dancing, puffs of dust rising from their pounding feet as they singly or in couples broke the circle to lean forward, stroking the lion's mane or smearing Mac's skin with a glutinous white paint smelling of rancid animal fat.

Dragging himself to his feet, Mac glanced down, unsurprised and accepting, as he discovered he was no longer wearing the cream twill jeans and blue gingham sports shirt he'd donned this morning.

Instead, except for a soft leather loincloth, he was as naked as the phantoms in the circle; his coffee-coloured skin was daubed with intricate patterns of white dots. As he shook his head to clear it, the lion-masked Rama stood before him. Taking his hand, Rama curled Mac's clumsy fingers around the smooth wood of a long hunting spear, its bone point wickedly sharp.

'Dance, my son, dance until you enter the great silence. Dance until you find the answers you seek from this land of your ancestors.'

Bewitched or becalmed by the fire coursing through his veins, solidifying in his gut where the cancer ate away at his spirit, Mac leapt into the centre of the circle with a strength he hadn't known he still had.

While the creatures from the walls danced on and off the corrugated tin sheets, while lions roared and antelopes thundered in ever smaller dust circles, men and women ululated as Mac stamped and pounded the earth, screaming out his sorrows and his regrets, his pain and his fears.

He shook his spear at the heaven he had never really believed in, the heaven and sky invisible through the smoke-filled room, where shards of light, thick with dust motes, danced to the rhythmic clapping of painted hands as painted mouths chanted encouraging words he could not understand, but could only feel rumbling through every cell in his body.

Mac twirled and twirled, his tawny leather loincloth flying and falling, flying and falling, until he felt the breath of an arcane god light the fire of life in him. Finally, the flames consumed him; he let go of his pain and his fears, and he fell … fell … fell into a silence so deep everything disappeared, and he simply floated in the darkness as Rama, and his painted living creatures faded into nothing...

One year later, Mackenzie Carter sat on the porch of his grandmother's house, down in McComb, Mississippi, watching the wind rustle through the old oak trees her grandfather had planted when he built the house in 1898. He saw Clint Jessop stop at the rickety old mailbox at the end of the twin strips of dirt drive to deliver the week's mail.

'Mornin', Mac,' Clint called as he noticed Mac with his feet up on the porch rail. 'Got an interestin' letter for you today.'

'Uh-huh,' Mac said, watching Clint walk up the drive.

'Yup.' Clint said, handing Mac a well-travelled envelope, the bold black and gold logo of a burning campfire almost obscured by water and dirt stains and various coloured postmarks. 'All the way from South Africa.'

Mac tapped the letter in the palm of his hand until, 'Ain't ya goin' to open it?' Clint asked.

'It's probably just promotional material,' Mac said. 'Nothing I can use here.'

Stroking a fingernail across the campfire logo, his mind edged towards that zone he'd found in a small tin shack in the land of his ancestors. The hotel doctor had said his fainting spell had been brought on by his illness, jet lag and dehydration, but Mac knew better.

'Well, open it already,' Clint said, impatient in his curiosity, and Mac opened the crumpled envelope, shivering as the memories rolled in.

As they returned to the sanitised hotel, he asked Rama to be his permanent driver for the two weeks he'd booked to stay in South Africa. Together, they'd travelled the country: from the legendary

Crook's Corner straddling three countries, South Africa, Zimbabwe and Mozambique in the far north, to the exquisite beauty of Table Mountain in the south.

He'd left Rama at the gate of Cape Town International Airport, shoving a wad of American dollars into his hands as both payment and tip and returned home, feeling better than he had in years but at peace and ready to die.

The weeks had become months, and still, he lived.

'The new scan shows you're all clear,' his oncologist said when Mac went for a check-up. 'There must be some mistake. We'll have to rerun it to—'

Mac had cut him off and returned home to McComb, where he'd become a regular worshipper at the rebuilt Temple Hill Missionary Baptist Church. There, as songs of praise bounced off the wood-panelled walls and the red silk banner, its gold lettering declaring WE SHALL NEVER TURN BACK, quivered in the lazy swirl of roof fans, he joined the dancing and the singing until he disappeared into another time, another space, where the chants were strange clicks, and the pounding heat carried the scent of blackcurrants and paraffin.

Shaking his head to clear it, he pulled out the letter and read:

Dear Mr Carter

I refer to Online Booking Number 54732 for one (1) driver and Class A vehicle (Mercedes Benz S class sedan or similar). Our driver, Mr Isaac Nkunthula, was present at OR Tambo International Airport on your expected arrival date. Our team was unable to contact you by email or mobile telephone. The hotel listed on your booking had no record of your stay.

Therefore, in terms of the South African Credit Act No 27 of 1995, you are hereby notified that, due to your non-appearance, you are liable for the total cost of R15 280, being said vehicle and driver from Sun Shuttle Services.

Kindly contact our credit department at accts@sunshuttle.co.za or Tel: +27 11 433 6597 to arrange payment.

Yours sincerely

PJ Naidoo
Credit Manager
Sun Shuttle Services

'Mac, Mac, are you okay? You're as white as my mammy's hair,' Clint said, whipping his cap off and fanning it in Mac's direction.

Mac ignored him. The letter fell into his lap, and as his head sank back against the hard oak of the rocking chair, Mac shut his eyes, fading out Clint and the sounds of a Mississippi morning so that he could better hear that familiar voice murmuring in his memory.

'*Ai! Ai!* Mr Car-tee-ay,' !XuRama said, 'I can take you to the heart of e'Goli, where the spirits of your ancestors live in the painted walls, and the city breathes with life.'

Life, Mac thought, is not only for the living but also for the dead.

And who — except, perhaps, the descendants of the ancient !XoiSan people still living in this ancient land — can ever know which is which?

Under Blue Waters

The beauty of discovering I am a mermaid is the freedom. The water lifts the weight of my tail, adding strength and power, as I breach the surface of the blue waters.

'Look at that!' The humans watching me from the shore clap in awe. My mother — also a human — claps the loudest of all, smiling and praising how I make my tail splash water so high droplets shower down like stars falling from the sky to land on the grey boulders corralling the sea into a protected cove.

Down, down, I dive, deep into the dark blue water. Still, I hear the muted calls of the humans, landlocked by their legs, while I swirl like a seal I once saw at the Ubuntu Marine World near Cape Town.

I watched the seal show from the beach — more a pile of fake rocks scattered along a slice of real sand leading into the seal pool. Near me, a barefoot young human dressed in baggy white shorts, his chest smooth and hairless, called the seals, who swam in fast, excited circles before approaching their trainer.

'Hi, Shrek,' the trainer greeted a large seal with long whiskers and odd-shaped ears. 'Oh, thank you, Amanzi,' he said to another smaller seal with a scar on her face. 'You brought me a leaf. Everybody clap for Amanzi,' urged the trainer. 'She's very shy about her scar.'

I laughed and laughed as the seal called Shrek splashed his trainer with water and honked. My laughter sounded just like Shrek's, and the little seal Amanzi swam up, curiously bumping the wheels of my chair with her wet nose. The trainer threw an ugly little glance in my direction. 'Ready, Amanzi,' he called, clapping his hands so that the seal slid into the water and swam back to him.

I disturbed him so much that I just sank back into my bubble.

There, sounds are muted, and no one's opinion of me can hurt. I'm safe, and they are comfortable again.

Some humans, like Mama, can see beyond my appearance. Even though they don't speak my language, even though they hear nothing but grunts and gasps when I sing or talk, they can understand what I'm saying.

Mama often boasts to her friends about how well I swim.

'I'm a mermaid,' I tell them. 'Of course, I can swim well. The water is my home, not this chair.'

As they sit there juggling their plates of red velvet cake and coffee cups, my mermaid senses pick up on those who, like the seal trainer, are disturbed by my presence. There are others, those whose children are fairies or unicorns, who, like Mama, nod and laugh and lean forward to touch my shoulder or my cheek when I talk.

I know, and they know, that all I say is lost in the translation from mermaid to human, but they do their best to treat me like they would anyone else.

So I hug them, wrapping my long arms and tail around them, squeezing tight, and laughing loudly when they hug me back.

'Careful, Miriam.' Mama jumps up to untangle my grip without hurting me.

She angers me, and I lash out, screaming, 'Maribel! My mermaid name is Maribel!'

Mama only wraps me deeper in her love and in her arms. 'You don't know your own strength, darling. Let go gently now.'

I slap my tail furiously, kicking the footrest, while I pound the arms of my chair with hands that are always dry and cold out of the water.

'Please, Miriam, please. Relax. This is doing no one any good!'

With my mermaid ears so finely tuned, I hear undertones that human ears can't fathom. Beneath the love always in Mama's voice, I hear that other constant thing: sorrow.

Mama never shows that part of herself to the disapproving human world with its narrow sense of what is beautiful or what is perfect. Mama knows, and her friends who have fairy and unicorn babies know, too, that beauty isn't the same for everyone. Only those who sail through life getting everything they want believe that beauty is no more than what the eyes see.

'Sally,' those petulant humans complain to Mama as she wipes my face where I missed my mouth while trying to eat my favourite snack, anchovy paste on toast. 'My holiday was so awful! Can you believe there were only two bathrooms? And we had to walk across a road to the beach!'

'That is disappointing,' says Mama, who hasn't had a holiday since I was born. Having a mermaid for a daughter, she says, is more important than being able to afford a holiday.

I've come to understand that in this world, there are those who, in their untouchable privilege, believe that they're entitled to a perfect life, and the perfect life they get is because they're so deserving, so good, and true. Their crippled souls are blinded by a naivety that can only understand their life, their pain, their truth.

These are the ones who look at us — the mermaids, the fairies, the unicorns — and see only that we don't fit into their little box of what beauty and truth are. They make token gestures of kindness that are not about what we need, but about what they need to look good in their own eyes, and in the eyes of the world they have moulded to their shallow, selfish limits, leaving us — the magical, the different, the dreamers — feeling less than them; feeling unheard, unseen, and unloved.

In the water, though, I am perfect. These humans, these creatures who play at kindness, are each ruled by wounds that, when triggered, make them the opposite of kind. Often, they justify their actions with excuses as shallow as a rain puddle, unable to see that I have my own kind of beauty simply because I'm a mermaid. In their eyes, I'm a mutant.

That's what Papa calls me the day he leaves us.

'She's a mutant!' Papa yells, standing at the door with his guitar and a rucksack over his shoulder. The keys to his motorbike rattle in the hand he shakes at Mama.

'She's your daughter too,' Mama says. 'She's part of you. How can you say that?'

'Look at her! Those…those…I can't even call them legs!'

'It's my mermaid tail,' I shout at Papa.

'Oh, God!' Papa says, his face twisting, his eyes hollow and his mouth nothing but an open cave with tangles of bitterness dripping like stalactites. 'Just listen to those noises!'

'You could understand me if you wanted to, Papa, but you don't listen!' As always, he ignores me, unable to see me for who I truly am.

I cry harder when Mama, her voice soft and calm, but her hand clutching mine so tightly it hurts, says, 'You could at least stay for Miriam's school play, Carl.'

'Mirabelle!' I shout. 'My name is Mirabelle!'

Papa, glaring at Mama, says, 'Are you mad? Miriam in the school play? It'll be a disaster! What can she be?'

'A mermaid,' Mama says.

'A mermaid, of course,' I say.

Papa snorts. 'Sally,' he says, his voice softer, almost kindly. 'There are homes for kids like this. She belongs in a home, where they know how to care for her. Let's find a place we can afford. We'll visit her,' he begs. 'Every day if you want. But at least we'll have some kind of normal life the rest of the time.'

His face is again the face of the Papa I remember when he used to lie on the floor with me on his chest, my arms— extra-long even then, an early sign of my mermaid-hood — waving in the air, reaching for the love on his face. 'She's going to be a bean pole, this one,' he would say, glowing with such love that my heart knew I'd always be safe with him.

Until the doctors discovered that I was growing into a mermaid.

Today his face blazes with a mix of emotions I can't name. I begin to cry, great gulping sobs, sounding like waves sucked back into the depths of the ocean as the tide drags the water through the jagged rocks protecting the cove where I'd first turned into a mermaid.

His finger, blunt and calloused from plucking his guitar, touches Mama's lips. 'Sally, do it for us.' His face crumbles, then goes still as he licks his lips, adding. 'Do it for her. She'll be happier in school with others like her.'

'No!' I scream. 'They'll lock me up in a pool. I'll never swim in the ocean again. I'll never feel my hair lifted by a seahorse hiding amongst the seaweed floating on the currents…'

I know the place he wants to send me. When I first transformed into a mermaid, Mama and Papa took me there week after week, as test after test was completed. The human doctors huddled over printouts and scans, looking concerned.

My transformation into a mermaid began long before I was born. Even before Mama and Papa were born, the mermaid seed was planted. My great-great grandma on Papa's side and my great-great grandpa on Mama's side had been amongst the first to leave the ocean to live as humans.

Those first ancestors of mine had beautiful human children, all ticking the beautiful box. They were perfect children through all the generations, but none ever felt the magic of their mermaid blood—until Mama and Papa fell in love. Then, the doctors said, in a one-in-seventy-million chance, the seed they each carried joined to birth me, the first mermaid in generations.

Unable to contain my heartbreak, my tail slaps the footrests. I use all my strength to throw myself onto the floor. Howling in frustration because I'm so useless on land, all I know is that I must reach him before he leaves us. So, like a crab I once watched in my ocean pool, I use my tail and my long arms in a kind of sideways shuffle and reach Papa in seconds before he even realises I'm coming.

'Don't go, Papa, don't go!' I plead, gripping his legs as hard as I can.

My tail flails around, knocking against the brown wooden table where Mama keeps a bowl of flowers and her favourite photograph, the one of Papa holding me as a newborn baby. He looks too young to be my Papa, with his long black hair and a beard covering half his face, but he still wears the same earring that glitters in the sunlit photograph, and the neck of his favourite guitar peers over his shoulder like a curious long-necked ostrich. His shining eyes, Mama always told me, were dreaming of walking me down the aisle one day because I was only a few weeks old and hadn't yet started to change into their miracle mermaid.

'Be careful, Miriam,' Mama cries, but she's too late.

On land, I can't control the power of my tailfins and they slice open like a broken pair of scissors. The photograph, in its silver and white frame, and the bowl of red-and-yellow flowers crash to the floor. Glass and water shatter, flying everywhere, cutting a deep gash in my left tailfin. Blood terrifies me, and as I see the dark red torrent, I scream, locking myself tighter to Papa. Mama tries to hold me still, pressing the tablecloth against the cut to stop the bleeding.

Papa glances down, his old guitar over his shoulder, his hair shorter and greyer than in the photograph I accidentally destroyed. Looking up from where I lie across his feet, I can see him swallow. He shakes his foot loose from my grip, his throat moving up and down as his face twists into something scary. 'I can't do this,' he says. 'This wasn't what I signed up for.'

'It's not what I signed up for either,' Mama screams. 'But it's what we've got. Can't you see? It doesn't matter that she can't move properly or that we can't understand her language.'

Mama drops the cloth she's pressing against the cut in my tailfin and wraps me in her arms. Her tears mix with mine as she says, 'She's ours. We made her.' Mama tickles my nose, as my sobs slow to gasps. 'She's beautiful. In her own way, she's more beautiful than other kids. She's always smiling. She's so full of love and when she's in the water—' Pride swells in Mama's voice. 'She outswims everyone. You can't even tell she's different.'

'I am different,' I say. A mermaid's job is to love everyone so much that we take away their pain. That's why our bodies are strange and twisted compared to the others; we carry their pain, so they don't have to.'

'I know, Miriam, I know, darling,' Mama says, wiping the wet hair away from my forehead.

She doesn't know. She still calls me Miriam, after her mother's mother, when I keep on telling her my mermaid's name is Mirabelle. I am sad that Mama can no more understand me when I speak than Papa can. All they hear are the grunts and snorts of my mermaid language, but at least Mama listens with her heart, while Papa listens only with his ears.

'Come to the water tank this afternoon, Carl,' Mama begs Papa. 'You'll see how she is in the water — you'll be so proud.'

Papa looks at Mama and then drops his sea-green gaze to where I lie, tangled on the floor, my tail flopping over Mama's jean-covered legs, wet now from all the water on the floor, his face unmoving until he gives one long, slow blink, shaking his head as if, like Rufus, Mrs Wilson next door's blind old dog, he is struggling to see what lies in front of him. For a long moment, none of us move, and then, without a word, Papa turns away, the door slamming shut behind him.

I do not want to go to the water tank that afternoon. When Papa left, my bubble of love collapsed. How will I be safe from the stares and sniggers of the swim team practicing in the Olympic-sized swimming pool at the gathering center? My heart is still sad, hanging heavy in my chest. Mermaids, I know, can't be sad. We must be happy all the time, otherwise our human family may abandon us, leaving us vulnerable and afraid in the hands of strangers.

I go to the tank practice with Mama, though, because I must be happy—happier than ever before— so that Mama will not want to leave me like Papa has.

A mermaid's job is to bring humans solace in their lives, lives so heavy with fear and anxiety about the darkness pressing ever closer. I felt that darkness reach out this morning when the door slammed behind Papa, leaving Mama and me on the floor, begging him not to go.

How can I go to the tank to practice for a joy show when I can't even bring my own Papa joy?

Not even the promise of dressing in my best blue tail, the one that sparkles and glitters as I undulate through the blue water makes me happy. I want the real ocean, with the fishy smell. The rough grains of sand squeeze through my fingers as, with Mama walking beside me, I drag myself to the water's edge, where the rocks curve into the small protected cove I lie in. Where I can laugh and laugh as gentle waves slosh over my tail fins, the rising wind tangles my hair around my ears, and even the strangers who hear only grunts and snorts rather than a mermaid's laughter will smile and say to Mama, 'She's having so much fun. What a happy soul she is, considering everything.'

'She loves the ocean,' Mama will answer.

I do love the ocean. The ocean is my real home, where I'm strong and free and as graceful as a sea ballerina, at one with all the creatures of the deep, safe in the swathes of seaweed that wrap me in warm, wet fingers of love. The ocean is so different from here, on this dry land, where I flop around like a gutted dying fish, and even my Papa—my own Papa—can't love or understand me.

Today, I want the ocean, not a glass tank that displays me to awkward human eyes, even if Mama is there clapping encouragement and Miss Elsa, too, my mermaid mentor, who first taught me how to swim and how to be a mermaid.

There is no escape. Perhaps Mama knows if she takes me to the ocean today, I'll escape into the

deep blue waters beyond my cove of calm water. I'll
wriggle across the ring of protective boulders and slip
easily into the water. In my natural element, with one
swish of my powerful tail, I will forever escape this
no-life in the human world. Perhaps Papa will return
to Mama and perhaps she will laugh again. And
perhaps I, too, will be free.

At the gathering place Mama and Miss Elsa
help me into my best mermaid tail: shimmering
turquoise with silver seashells jangling at the waist.
They slip my arms into the sleeves and tug the top
into position so that the two silver seashells cover my
changing chest. Mama outlines my eyes with silver
and turquoise waterproof makeup while Miss Elsa
pins a piece of purple coral into my hair.

Then it is time.

They help me to the edge of the tank. 'Take a
deep breath like I taught you, Miriam,' Miss Elsa
says.

'Mirabelle!' I grunt. I don't wait for her reply
because, even though it wasn't the ocean, even though
no sea creatures lived in this tank as they do in
aquarium tanks, the water is still my home, the place
where I'm as graceful and beautiful on the outside as
Mama says I am on the inside.

As I scull through the heavy water, I see a
mirage of Papa standing by my empty chair. The pain
is too much, and, as Miss Elsa taught me, I press my
tongue against the roof of my mouth to stop myself
from panicking and gulping water.

Closing my eyes to block out the impossible
dream, I sink slowly downwards, a small stream of air
bubbles escaping through my nose. I twist into a
graceful barrel roll and my hair floats out behind me,
gently waving in the water until my tail thumps on the
bottom of the tank.

I open my eyes to get my bearings and Papa is
still there. He has moved so that his hands push

against the tank's glass as tears stream down his cheeks. I can't hear the words, but I can read his lips, 'Miriam,' he chants silently. 'Miriam!'

Out of the depths of the deep blue water, I smile. A few more bubbles of air escape and, with a powerful mermaid kick, I swim to the glass wall, placing the palms of my hands against Papa's hands pressed so tightly against the glass. My eyes drift shut so I can't see the pain in his. Dreamily, I float forward and kiss him through the cold, clear barrier of glass, but when I open my eyes again, Papa is gone.

My lungs begin to burn, demanding oxygen. Miss Elsa says I've stayed under the water too long when my lungs feel like they'll burst. This time, it isn't a lack of air that attacks my lungs, but grief—grief that, by being who I am and what I am, I chased Papa out of our lives. What use am I, then, if even being a mermaid isn't enough to make my Papa love me?

I want to stay under, to open my mouth and let the water fill my lungs until all the pain is gone, for becoming a mermaid is too hard, too false a hope to carry: an illusion I can no longer believe.

Rippled by the water above me, I see two faint outlines at the edge of the tank. Mama and Miss Elsa. Mama waves her arms, beckoning me to the surface. What would Mama do without her mermaid to bring her joy if I let go? I blink once, twice. Using all the strength in my arms to lift my crippled body, made heavier by the deadweight of the mermaid tail Mama made with so much love, I surge through the blue water, bursting through the surface, air gasping into my lungs, blue streams sluicing off my shoulders as Miss Elsa, lying flat along the tank edge, her hands outstretched, grabs my hands, keeping me afloat.

There are still two figures standing next to the tank: Mama and, next to her, Papa.

'How is it possible?' he asks, his voice hoarse and low. 'How is it possible that a child so physically disabled can move like that in the water?'

'Because I'm a mermaid, Papa,' I shout gleefully, splashing my hands on the water, making waves that splash Miss Elsa in the face and wet Papa's legs and shoes. Mermaid mischief, Miss Elsa calls it.

'Miriam,' he cries, dropping to his knees on the boarding platform edging the hydrotherapy tank. 'My baby love, I'm sorry! I'm sorry! Papa will never leave you again!'

Pushing Miss Elsa aside, he grabs my hands and pulls me towards him. Happiness spills over into mischief, and I lean back into the water so that Papa overbalances, falling into the tank, making the biggest splash ever.

When he surfaces next to me, I'm buoyant enough in the water for him to lift me over his shoulder. I slap my mermaid tail until the water is everywhere, streaming off Mama and Miss Elsa, as Papa holds me tight and says, 'Oh Miriam, what am I going to do with you?'

I hear both the love and sorrow in his voice. As I watch the water stream off his hair, dribbling through his earring in sparkling droplets, I laugh and laugh, grunting and snorting without a care in the world, for with Papa back and Mama standing there in soaked jeans and t-shirt, I know this one truth: some people, ignorant of the miracles love performs, might think I am disabled, trapped for a lifetime in a useless body over which I have so little control.

But Mama knows, and now Papa knows, too: mermaids are real; they exist to bring love and laughter, happiness and hope into a world that has forgotten that miracles happen in the most magical ways.

And I am a mermaid.

The Wedding

Margo made me wait a full year before she said yes.

I met her in a bar, slumped on a barstool, looking sad and scared. The brute beside her was overly friendly — one hand up her skirt and the other methodically tossing cheap whisky back. His remarks became wilder and cruder as the hand under her skirt worked harder and faster.

My Margo just sat there, getting limper and limper as he played her. When his hand stopped tossing back the whisky and started unzipping his trousers — right there, in the public bar, as if she wasn't worth even the slightest courtesy! — it became too much for me to bear.

'Doll,' I said, putting my hand on the brute's wrist and dragging it from under her lacy skirt. 'Is this palooka bothering you?'

She didn't answer. She looked at me with those great sad eyes, half-covered by her dirty blonde hair.

'Fuck off,' the brute said. 'I bought her. I can do anything I want with her, and there ain't nothing you can do about it.'

For the last year, I'd trained every day in the gym, so I knew how to flex my muscles. 'Try me,' I said and squeezed his wrist harder.

'Aaaaah, fuck!' he said. 'If she means so much to you, she's yours. She was cheap enough.' He pushed her towards me, quick as a snake, so that my beautiful Margo landed in a heap at my feet, bedraggled hair hiding those sad, sad eyes.

'Come,' I said, picking her off the floor as if she were a wounded kitten.

My new apartment, the one I'd moved into a year ago, was above the bar. Although small, there was enough room to bathe her and wash her hair until it shone like a golden halo. Still, she stayed silent, gazing at me as if expecting me to treat her as a worthless piece of trash, an unwanted sex toy of no value to anyone, even herself.

'What's your name, Doll?' I asked, brushing a golden strand away so she couldn't hide and I could stare more deeply into her weary, wary eyes.

Then, as softly as a mother sings a lullaby to a child, she said, 'Margo. Call me Margo.'

Moved beyond words by her courage and her vulnerability, I could only begin to make sweet love to her, each soft squeak she made telling me that she, too, felt this moment as deeply as I.

She never left after that night. Soon, people grew used to seeing us together. As I worked the bar, settling drunken disputes and keeping order, she'd sit on the same barstool I first saw her. Safe under my protection, no one ever bothered her.

'Hello, Yuri,' they'd say. 'Hello, Margo.' I'd greet the regulars with a wave, but Margo — who felt no shyness when talking to me in our modest apartment — would sit silently waiting for me.

Every time we made love, I'd beg her. 'Marry me, Margo. I can't live without you.'

Always, she just stared at me. Not wanting to hurt me, she never said no, but never said yes, either.

One glorious spring day, as we lay in a patch of bluebells, our nakedness dappled by the dense forest foliage, I asked her again.

To my delight — my amazement — she buried her face in my shoulder and, on a breath that whistled gently out of her, she said, 'Yes, Yuri, yes. I will marry you.'

The wedding was small and intimate, with only Joe, my boss, the bar owner, his wife Patty, a few friends from the gym, and a stranger.

A slender young man in ripped jeans, a t-shirt covered in angry slogans rising out of a nuclear mushroom cloud and a camera. No one owned up to calling the press, but I let him stay for Margo looked so beautiful in her white lace dress, a row of tiny pearl buttons down the back, the décolletage perhaps a little low for a wedding dress, but I liked it, and that was all that mattered to Margo.

Our wedding photos went viral, and my X account exploded with followers. Some requested photos of Margo, others wanted to know more about her personality, and others enjoyed hearing about our love story.

I was so proud, but my Margo hated the fame our wedding brought her. 'Yuri,' she'd whisper in that still quiet voice. 'My nose isn't right.'

It wasn't, but I told her I loved her just as she was. As I ran my hand over her luscious bosom, she'd cry, 'My ta-tas are too small.' They were, but I told her I loved her as she was.

On and on that insidious voice went until I could no longer bear to see her so sad.

I added up my bank balance. I asked Joe if I could work extra shifts in the bar. I sold my bicycle, even though it was less than a year old. I'd only bought it after I smashed my Ferrari in the accident. Eventually, I had enough money to make Margo happy.

'Come, Margo,' I said, and we walked to the nearest clinic. Everyone said Dr van Bergen was the best surgeon in the city.

He looked surprised when I walked in, his eyes sliding to Margo before quickly returning to me.

'Hello, Dr van Bergen,' I said, shaking his hand before introducing him to Margo. 'This is my wife, Margo. She's your patient today.'

He, too, clearly thought Margo was perfect as she was, for his face had a stunned look that reminded me of a dog that's chased a car, caught it and then doesn't know what to do with it.

'Yuri,' he said, avoiding looking at Margo by straining to keep his gaze locked on mine. 'I couldn't possibly operate on your wife…on Margo.'

I stood up, leaning on his desk with my fists. Sensing my building fury, Margo squeaked in dismay as I moved.

'Why not?' I snarled. 'It's what she wants.' I leaned in closer, knowing my size alone is menacing. 'What I want.'

'Yuri,' he said, not budging an inch. 'I can't operate on Margo. She's dead.'

'No, she's not.'

'Your wife died two years ago, Yuri. Don't you remember? There was nothing I could do after the car accident. The burns were too severe.'

'She's here,' I shouted, pointing to my Margo, sitting so quietly in the chair. 'She's right here!'

He pressed the intercom on his desk, murmuring, 'Bring me 50mLs of Haldol Decanoate, IM. And that's stat, Carla.'

He stood up and walked around his desk, his coat brushing a silver-framed photograph of his wife and three children, the vast empty ocean spread out behind their happy faces.

He reached me and said, 'I'm sorry, Yuri, but that's not Margo.' Gently, he touched my hand. 'That's a doll, a plastic sex doll.'

I picked my Margo up from the chair where she flopped, her painted eyes staring unblinkingly as I shook her in his face.

'It's Margo,' I sobbed. 'It's Margo!'

I was still sobbing her name as he pushed the needle into my arm, and the world went blessedly black…

In the Country of the Free

Prologue

*As far back as our memory goes — to the last
millennia, the last month — we can remember the
great migrations. The herds of wildebeest in the
Serengeti searching for sweet new grass. The shoals
of sardines that run under the warm waters of
Southern Africa. And a seething mass of humanity ...
ah, we humans journey far to escape the horrors of
our homelands in an elusive search for freedom.*

Part 1: The Homeland – Na'omi (14 years old)

Their hearts as black as the night just ended,
they burst from the jungle, rampaging through our
village, only their war-fevered eyes visible beneath
the black-and-white striped keffiyehs covering their
heads.

We scattered before their stamping feet, the
rapid bullet fire almost drowning the anguished cries
of our parents. Draped with machetes, machine guns
and belts of bullets, Boko Haram swarmed over the
unfenced schoolyard like hungry locusts.

My mother — descended, she often said, from
a warrior tribe — was the only parent who thundered
after us. Her green dress, with its broad orange leaves
boldly decorating the skirt, flapped against her legs as
she ran towards us, clasping my youngest brother, not
yet three months old, to her left hip. In her right hand,
she clutched the new broom she'd finished making

after church last week: her only weapon against the men herding us back into the dense bush, away from all we'd ever known.

In another time, another place — perhaps tucked into my bed, Mama kneeling next to me, stroking the nightmares away with her stories of our ancestors and their warrior strength — I would have laughed for she looked so funny: Chomo squalling, toothless gums wide as he bounced up and down on her hip as she ran, shaking the straw broom at the man dragging me away.

I could not laugh, though, for his grip on my arm was so tight I cried with pain, choking on the mix of dust and snot and tears running down my face.

As Mama reached us, she hit him so fiercely that his hold loosened, and I fell into the dirt. A sharp crack and Mama screamed, falling next to me in the dirt, her arm flung loosely over my back, her broom snapped in two, spinning harmlessly out of her hand.

At that moment, I was safe again, so safe that I could no longer hear Chomo's screams as he lay tucked between Mama and me. Before I could do more than call Mama's name, the man kicked her aside and, hurling me over his shoulder, carried me away from the village I'd never once left before that day.

Beyond our village border, three open-sided trucks were waiting. 'Get in! Get in!' they shouted, but some girls were too frightened to climb up the high-sided vehicle.

Shoving a rifle against Ladi's head, the leader screamed louder, 'Get in! In the name of Allah, get in, or I'll shoot!'

Afraid of dying, we scrambled up into the truck closest to us. We travelled for hours along an open road in the dark, and thinking it would help the police find us, I carefully let my headscarf slip off my head and over the edge of the truck. In a whisper, I told the other girls what I'd done. Soon, they, too, let their headscarves drop when the guards weren't looking.

We drove for several days through dry wastelands, the trucks kicking up dust like a suffocating, arid fog swirling across fields of blackened trees. We drove on over rivers that nearly drowned us, days of endless driving until, at last, we disappeared into a thick, dark forest.

Later, when we had not been moved again for days, the girls spoke of my mother.

'She is dead,' said Blessings. Unbraiding her hair, she spoke as if Mama were a fly swatted by the casual hand of a giant. 'She was shot.'

'She tripped,' I said, ignoring the memory of how loosely her hand had landed across my shoulder blades, 'and she had no breath to cry out after her fall.'

'Your mama was brave,' Abigail, the youngest of us, said, her hand creeping into mine. 'My mama can't love me as much as your mama loves you.'

She hid her face in my arm so only I knew she was weeping, her tears warm rivulets through the red dust clinging to my skin. Crowded together in a half-burnt church, we'd not been allowed to bathe yet. Late at night, when all was silent, we heard the sound of water and knew there was a stream nearby, but there was no running water in our prison; they had brought us only one large container of water; we had barely enough to drink and did not know when they would bring the next one.

None of us knew where we were. I'd caught glimpses of the village where we were being held captive. Surrounded by a mix of dense trees, not much taller than me, and thorny bushes, it looked different from our village. No one had said anything about the black-and-white flag flying from a rough wooden pole hastily planted in the ground, so I didn't say anything either, wanting to believe that we were still near our homeland.

Putting my arms around Abigail, I sat down and stroked her forehead as Mama had stroked mine. 'Of course, your mama loves you,' I said. 'Why would you think not?'

'She didn't try and save me, like your mama.'

Blessings snorted. 'Be glad your mama's not as stupid as Na'omi's mama,' she said. 'Dead mamas can't go to the police and send them to rescue us.'

The police did not come. No one came except the men who had stolen us. First, they stripped us of our blue-and-white checked school dresses, the yellow badge over our left breast boldly stating our school's name, our last reminder of where we had come from.

As we stood in front of the remains of the altar, we huddled together to hide our nakedness from their greedy, glittering eyes and from the unseen eyes of our God. Then, the men each chose a bride for the night. I could see little of my "husband" — his head, his body, was covered in black, the only colour a gold ring glinting on the hand that held his gun; I had seen it when he captured me after he'd made my mother fall in the dirt the day they stole us away.

That night, our wedding night, they called it, the rebel used me the way a man uses his wife. I fought him silently, calling in my heart to the blood of my warrior mother and my mother's people that ran in my veins.

'You're as foolish as your mother,' he said that first night. 'You're lucky I don't teach *you* to be silent,' he added, pushing me face down in the dirt, 'like I taught that dirty screaming cow that birthed you!'

Then he took me as a bull takes its cow. That first night was the only night I cried, so I was glad to lie in the dirt, my damp face hidden from his stinking body and his dead brown eyes. Never again did I cry when he, or one of the others, took me, for I would not shame my mama by again showing fear.

The following day, we were taken to the stream we'd heard but not seen. I stood next to Blessings, no longer the sharp-tongued, bright-eyed girl ruling over our village playground, but a fragmented shadow: her one eye swollen shut and her perfect front teeth broken off at the gum, the wounds on her back and legs still weeping around bruises shaped like boot treads.

She'd always been our leader, but today, ignoring the blood and filth that soldier had left on me from the wedding night none of us had chosen, I washed Blessing as I had watched my mama wash Chomo when he was a day-old babe. With a touch so gentle it almost didn't exist, I spoke of her dreams of going to university to study nursing, of her boyfriend who called her the centre of his world, and of the new blouse with the gold thread and silver beads, her aunt had sent her from England. I spoke without waiting for an answer, for Blessings had none to give except the unspoken words swimming in the tears that dripped from the corners of her swollen eyes.

After I had led Blessings to a flat rock on the edge of the river bed, I returned to the water to wash myself. But Abigail stood before me, then Ruth, then Elinor, and I washed and washed them all until our girlhood and the dreams we had once had been scrubbed clean. Then, at last, I had only myself left to cleanse.

We became faceless after our wedding night when our husbands handed us bride clothes.

'Here is the dress of a modest woman,' they said, pointing to a pile of black hijabs. 'You will wear these before the imam arrives.'

We dressed quickly, awkward with the unfamiliar clothing and nervous under their dark, hungry gazes as they leaned against the trees on the riverbank. 'Sit here,' they ordered, arranging us like dolls in a half circle. 'Keep your eyes modest,' they added, 'and read these holy words of Allah.'

They gave us each a book written in a strange language we could not understand. When they were satisfied that we had done what they wanted, they took a video on their leader's cell phone and photographs to send to our families and the world to show them how happy we were, with such devout men to protect our honour and save our souls from our previous lives as infidels.

'We must obey,' I said to the other girls later that night after we'd eaten the few handfuls of rice and beans we had as our daily meal. 'Obey and live. The photos will give clues on where we are. Our parents will send the police, or they will find a way to pay a ransom, but we won't be forgotten,' I promised. 'My mama will never let us be forgotten.'

I knew that, at least, was true, and quietly, so quietly my voice was almost silent, I led them in a prayer to our God.

Twelve full moons have faded into the midnight sky. I am now the leader's wife, for Blessings, his chosen wife, was soon pregnant. I tried my best, but she lost the baby, and soon after, we lost her — it was then he decided I must be his. He put me in charge of the cooking and nursing duties when the soldiers returned from their hunts, and I also became the "mother" of the girls.

The girls still come to me with their problems, but they have long ago stopped believing my promise that the police will come, that my mama will find a way to fetch us home. I, too, falter at times and weep when no one is awake. Then I remember my mama, her grass broom slicing the air as dangerously as the sharpest machete as she alone tried to stop them from stealing us. For as long as she still draws breath, such a woman, I know, will not give up.

As I stir and stir the cooking rice, the water bubbling with the same heat that swells my heart with renewed hope, I promise myself that I, her daughter, will never stop dreaming of the freedom that awaits us when, one day, we return to the homeland we yearn for every day the sun still rises over the black-and-white flag staked in the centre of the camp.

In the Country of the Free

Part 2: The Journey – Amira (3 years old)

We left Bab al-Salameh as the night began, the pink-blue sky fading into the tops of the tents. Mohammed, my husband, is a good man: by begging, borrowing, perhaps stealing, but mostly by working at the menial tasks no one else wants to do, he saved four thousand American dollars to pay the smugglers to take us across the Turkish border. We'll go overland to Bodrum and catch the boat to Farmakonisi; after that ... America, where Mohammed's uncle's second cousin by marriage has family willing to take us in and help us start a new life.

Before we left our homeland, Mohammed owned three tailor shops in Aleppo: the small shop in the souk he inherited from his father, who had inherited from his father before him; the others Mohammed had built up on his own, sometimes employing as many as five people. From those profits, Mohammed bought us a house facing south, with an inner courtyard, which I filled with climbing jasmine and three white rosebushes next to the small corner fountain. The cool stone floor was decorated with geometric blue-and-white tiles, and I would sit under the potted lemon tree, watching our daughters play.

Amira, the younger, was our beauty: her short brown hair framing her face, her chocolate eyes holding all the ancient mysteries of the world, reflecting green flecks when she wore her favourite lime green dress, with tiny frills ruched around the neck and arm lines. Boldly splashed in pink and white and blue flowers, she would wear it as often as possible.

She'd stand in our small courtyard, chubby legs planted firmly on the ground, one star-shaped hand on her hip, the other pointing imperiously at her sister. Layaali, our eldest, all growing arms and spindly legs, would uncomplainingly re-arrange dolls and tea glasses under the direction of her sister.

When the bombs first started falling, we stayed. We stayed when our house had no running water, and the courtyard tiles were broken and scattered. We stayed until the day Mohammed came home, his face pale beneath the blackness of his beard, his trousers streaked with blood and dirt.

'Yara,' he said to me, pushing my hands away as I felt his legs for the bleeding wounds, 'that is not my blood.'

'Whose blood is it, then?' I asked, sitting back on my haunches, looking up at him and wondering at the tear tracks on his cheeks.

'I don't know, Yara! She was a child! A girl not much older than our Amira.' He gulped deep sobs back, then buried his face in his hands. 'I passed her on my way to deliver Mr Aflaq's new shirts; she was drawing pictures of trees in the sand with a stick. I saw them — I saw them taking bets. If I'd known—' He broke off and took hold of my shoulders, his fingers digging deep as he looked at me with eyes that had seen what they should not see.

'If you'd known what, Mohammed?' I asked gently, ignoring the pain where his fingers burrowed into my flesh, reaching up to clasp his wrist in my hand.

'The bet...the bet was to see who could shoot her. He was a boy himself, Yara – the winner! He just slung the rifle off his shoulder and shot her, laughing when he took the prize money. I ran to see if I could help her, but she was dead. Four years old, and she died in the dirt at the hands of another child.'

I began wailing in concert with his grief, flinging my apron over my face. But I could not hide from the sorrow that invaded our lives that day.

Mohammed stood up. 'We're going to America, Yara – you and me and the girls,' he said.

As damaged as they were, I didn't want to leave my country or my house. 'When will we leave?' I sobbed, hoping he would change his mind before we actually had to leave.

'Tonight,' he said, ignoring me as I wailed louder, falling on my knees before him, begging him to wait a month or two before taking us away from all we knew.

'We leave tonight,' he said, turning away from me, his heart as hard as the stones once used to decorate the courtyard floor I loved so much. 'Pack only the essentials for you and the girls. I'll pack for myself later.'

'Where are you going?'

'I have the cash I've been saving in the shops; I'm going to fetch it — we need it now, not in the future.'

By the time he returned home, Amira, dressed in her favourite green flower dress, was in a temper, clinging to her dolls and her tea set, refusing to leave them behind. Her father made her choose and then carried her tea set in his rucksack all through the days it took us to reach the border.

Mohammed's savings were quickly spent once we lived in Bab al-Salameh, but we survived. In the long months it took for Mohammed to earn the extra American dollars we needed to continue our journey, Layaali never moved far from my side, but Amira … Amira soon won over the other children.

She'd spend her days spreading out her tea glasses, directing them where to sit, and then serving them her imaginary tea and sweetmeats. Even as it faded from too much wear, her dress became the only bright colour in a world filled with open sewerage, trash, and a sour haze that constantly choked us.

The evening we slipped out of the camp, running through trenches to avoid the coiled razor wire and the Turkish border guards, we were met by a driver who kept his face hidden. He drove us through the long night, only speaking to instruct us to lie flat to avoid being seen by a passing car. Arriving near Bodrum, nearly a full day later, he left us alone in a citrus orchard.

'Here is safe,' he said, driving us deep into the sweet-smelling trees. 'You stay here until I fetch tonight.'

The girls, exhausted from the tension and the long drive, slept peacefully under the thick shade of the orange trees. Mohammed and I could not rest until, hours later, we heard the truck through the darkness.

Arriving at the cove, the moon was bright enough for us to see the waiting boat. Bulkier than I expected, painted in two shades of blue, shining silver in the moonlight, the large rust patches along the sides turned into shadows creeping below the water line. Except for the Captain's cabin, painted white with three large windows and stairs leading up to a small, flat roof, the deck was open, unprotected from the weather. A few hollow metal pipes were loosely welded together and crisscrossed overhead so passengers had something to cling to during the crossing.

Already crowded, there were other new arrivals needing a place on board.

'You,' said the Captain. He pointed to Mohammed, his eyes counting how many passengers our family had. 'Where's your ticket money?'

'I paid for a small boat with only ten people,' Mohammed said. 'This boat is a danger for the passengers.'

'It's the only boat I've got,' said the Captain. A stout Greek, his shirt open to his waist, his gold Christian cross hung on his chest, twisting and turning as he moved. 'Get on board, or find another boat.'

'Do you have life jackets for us?'

'Another two hundred and fifty American dollars each. One hundred and fifty each for a tyre.'

'I don't have that much money,' Mohammed, stiff with frustration, said.

'Then you get on board or go.' The Captain dug into his shirt pocket and lit a cigarette, his eyes squinting through the smoke as he took money from another family.

Mohammed was angry, but I convinced him to do nothing: we had come so far, lost so much already, and had nowhere else to go except onto the boat and over the Aegean to Greece and then to America.

We didn't wait too long to board: the sea, already impatient with the delay, churned her waves higher as the boat sank lower with every extra body that climbed aboard.

We could not swim, but Mohammed protected us as he always did. Gathering Amira and Layaali in his arms, telling me to hold onto his jacket, he forced his way through the seething mass and secured a safe space for us on the small deck atop the Captain's cabin.

When the last of the arrivals had clambered on board, we set sail. I murmured a prayer to Allah, unable to stop my belly twisting with an uneasy mix of fear, hunger and excitement. In less than an hour, we would be free: free to live and work in peace, free from the gnawing fear that Mohammed would one day walk into our courtyard with one of our daughters lifeless in his arms.

The four of us sat together as the shore faded from view until we were surrounded by nothing but the wide waters heaving with white waves. Afraid, I peered at Mohammed in the darkness, the shadows wiping away the lines of care and darkening the silver at his temples so he was once again the handsome man I'd married.

'Sleep, my heart, sleep,' he whispered as I closed my eyes, leaning against his shoulder, his beloved face engraved into my memory. 'The girls already dream of our new life.'

In my restless dreams, my fears took over with a strange silence in which I could no longer hear the engines. The boat began to rock; raised voices became panicked cries, and the sounds of children weeping seared through the darkness.

The deck we sat on became slippery; no one could get a grip, and we tumbled helplessly over strangers as, even in my dream, I clung tightly to Mohammed, believing his hoarse whisper, 'Don't worry, Yara, I've got you, I've got the girls,' but as he spoke, the boat shuddered and trembled, tossing us off its decks as easily as a whirlwind tossed a leaf covered in dozens of clinging ants into a rain puddle, sucking the breath from their insignificant souls as water, salty as the sea, poured in to drown my desperate cry, 'Mohammed … Moham—'

Mohammed al-Noury and twenty-seven other sodden souls were rescued by the Greek Coast Guard, pulled from the angry waters like the human flotsam they were. The bodies of his wife, Yara, and their daughter, Layaali, together with another thirty-one passengers, were lost to the sea.

An old fisherman found Amira. He thought, at first, she was alive. But the movement that caught his attention on that pristine beach was only her lime-green dress, with its bold pink and white and blue flowers, fluttering in the breeze as she lay face down in the sand, her lifeless body cradled by the blue Aegean sea.

In the Country of the Free

Part 3: The Free – Hope (7 years old)

The sky is clear blue, the air bright with the rising sun when Hope pulls aside the gingham curtain, once red-and-white, now faded with age into a dull pink-and-grey.

Laughing, she calls to her maame, 'The day is beautiful! Can we go to the lake?'

Hope knows, on days like this, Maame will dress first Hope, then herself, in a rush. She'll leave the breakfast dishes unwashed in the green plastic bowl she keeps in the cupboard and fills with water from the garden tap. At night, they bathe, dipping a small hand towel into the water in the same bowl and rinsing their bodies until they're clean and sweet-smelling. Even in the winter, when the cold winds blow the snow in from northern England, Maame insists they bathe daily.

'We're poor, not pigs,' she would say, her teeth chattering with cold.

Today, though, is warm, the kind of day Maame says reminds her of her homeland. She was only fourteen when she left Ghana. Recently orphaned, she thought she was going on holiday, but her aunt left her with a family in London. For years, Maame cooked and cleaned for them, but when she asked for pay, they said they'd paid her aunt, and she could go to The Authorities if she wanted more.

Maame says The Authorities never help people like us; we have no papers. If they catch us, they'll send us back to Ghana, where we'll starve.

Despite the dangers, Maame is lonely for her homeland. Today, as they do each time weather and time allows, they sit together at the side of the lake and watch the cheeky ducks and graceful swans start the day. She cuddles into Maame's lap while Maame talks about walking along warm white beaches, past colourful wooden boats to sit under swaying palm trees haggling with fishermen over the price of a freshly caught fish.

Hope likes Maame's stories. Not that she wants to go to Ghana because she'll miss her friends here, but because, when she speaks of it, Maame's face softens, and she looks younger and prettier. That's how Hope knows about Maame's loneliness because, most times, Maame just looks tired and scared.

There is only ever the time for one story, for they cannot stay long at the lake. Maame must drop Hope off at school early because her shift at the Burger Bar and Grill starts at 07h00 sharp.

Maame's friend Ruth fetches Hope from school; she takes her home and helps with her homework. Today, Hope wants to stay outside in the warm sun.

'I want to say hello to Maame,' she says, dragging her feet when Ruth tries to turn into their street.

'You know Maame's too busy.'

'Please, Ruthie, please! I got a gold star today! I want to show Maame!'

Eventually, Ruth gives in to her pleas and takes her to the Burger Bar.

'Hello, Maame, hello,' Hope shouts as she sees her mother serving plates piled high with chips and burgers to two people at a table.

Maame looks so surprised, Hope just giggles and giggles. Then, noticing the badge Maame wears, she asks, 'Why are you called Ruth today?'

Maame rolls her eyes at a man standing near the door, watching. 'I'm only Maame to you, love because I'm your Mum.'

Hope is a clever girl and isn't satisfied. 'But your other name is Pa—'

'I gave your Mum my badge to wear because she borrowed my papers,' Ruth whispers, then urges Hope past the now-scowling man. 'Look,' she says loudly, 'I've found £2! Let's order some French fries!'

Soon, her nose buried in the rare treat of a packet of crisp hot chips, Hope forgets about Maame wearing Ruth's badge until that night when Maame comes home early.

'Ruth,' Maame cries, 'Oh God, Ruth, we have to move again! Tonight!'

She runs to the cupboard, nearly tripping over Hope, where she sits playing with her Bah-by. Hope had found the doll in a rubbish bin. With beautiful long blonde hair, blue eyes, and one leg missing, Bah-by had carried a doll-sized pink handbag with her name "Barbie" printed in glittering gold. Hope loves Bah-by and always does her homework better if Bah-by sits with her.

When Hope sees the tears on Maame's face and how her hands are shaking, she also starts weeping. She's not sure why, but she knows this happy day is changing.

'What is it, Patricia?' Ruth jumps up, spilling tea down her jeans.

Maame ignores her and pulls their clothes from the cupboard, shoving them into a plastic bag until Ruth grabs her wrist and shakes it. 'Stop panicking, Pat — tell me what's happening!'

Maame takes a few deep breaths and leans against the cupboard door. It's not really a cupboard; it's just a big box Maame bought home from the Burger Bar one night. She half-cut one side to make a door, and together, they painted it with bright colours, calling it their cupboard.

'Joseph knows I have no papers.' She drops the plastic bag onto the floor, dropping her head on Ruth's shoulder. 'Last week he said the customers like me because I'm always friendly! Now he'll ask for my passport to check against papers I don't have!'

'Are you sure, Pat? What did he say?'

'Nothing yet! But after you and Hope left, he asked me where Hope was born and who her father is...'

'Maybe he was being friendly? Getting to know you?'

'I can't take the chance!' Maame pulls away from Ruth and turns to kick a hole in the cupboard. 'OhGod! OhGod! Why do we have to move again? Mrs. Barnes says Hope is doing so well at school; she's happy there. I've been happy at the Burger Bar! Why can't they leave us alone? We're not stray dogs looking for someone to feed us! Why can't they realise we just want to work, to make a better life for our kids?'

'They think we're all terrorists,' Ruth says, scooping up Hope's grey jersey, the one with the red mice running along the bottom, which has fallen through the hole in the cupboard. 'Where will you go?'

'I'll stay in Manchester,' Maame says. Wrapping her arms around Hope's shoulder, she pats the soft, curly hair with agitated strokes. 'At the church shelter. Hope can stay in school for a few days while I find another job.'

'And if you can't, Pat?' Ruth asks, crossing her arms across her belly, stilling her restless fingers by clasping her elbows tightly. 'What then? You'll leave most of your stuff behind. You'll have to start all over again — with nothing!'

'Not nothing, Ruth,' Maame says, sounding calm and strong again. 'Even if I have nothing else left in this world, I'll always have Hope.'

Escaping the Thunderbolt

'Isaac,' Ma called over the baby's yell, 'don't go outside without me!'

The brightly coloured grasshopper was far more alluring than Ma's usual refrain. It hopped onto the windowsill where he sat gazing at the mysterious clumps of Lowveld beyond the rickety wire fence, which leaned haphazardly toward the winding dirt road to the farm.

'*Crrt! Crrt!*' he'd heard, and then it was there: the black armoured body with its bold bands of yellow, orange, and blue; the square head with two long black-and-orange antennae twitching this way and that; and the six striped legs.

As it waited for him, he slid the window open, working the sash as quietly as possible so Ma wouldn't hear. The creature grew impatient and took off in a blur, settling just outside the gate on the gnarled old Nyala tree, its trunk split in two by lightning long before Isaac was born. Worried it would leave without him, he tossed a quick glance over his shoulder to check Ma was still with the baby before dropping first one leg, then the other, over the sill to land with a quiet thump on the withered grass below.

'Hello, hopper,' Isaac said, cautiously opening the gate so it wouldn't squeak and warn Ma.

He walked to the Nyala tree with his hand outstretched, but before he could touch it, the insect stopped its vigorous crunching and, with a single thrust of its powerful hind legs, hopped up and flew clumsily from the tree to a bush and then onto another. Chortling at this new game, Isaac followed it as it disappeared so deep into the bushes that he couldn't see the roof of the house anymore.

All he could see and feel were the haze of the sun and the dust motes in the air that rose as his shoes scuffed the sand, dry because the rains were late. He forgot Ma had said the bush was dangerous; for now, his gaze was fixed firmly on the grasshopper. There was no danger in his mind, only the sound of his breathing and the sense of freedom until he was one with the still cacophony of the bush: the "go-way, go-way" caw of the grey *loeries*, the rustle of the rising wind through the thickets and the fading '*Crrt!*' of his friend, the grasshopper.

'Stop,' he panted as it leapt ahead again and again until he slowed to a stumbling walk because he could no longer see its rainbow legs or hear anything except the groan of the looming bushes and trees.

'Where are you?' he called, trying hard to stop the tears from gathering. Isaac wiped a grimy hand over his cheek and bent to pull up one of his socks. Ma would be mad when she saw how dirty he was, he thought, when — he gulped — if he ever made it home.

Slowly, he twirled around in a circle. He was almost a man, he knew, but his heart stuttered wildly as he saw that the dust no longer danced in the sunbeams and the sky had turned the dull grey of the battleship Pa had taken him to visit when last they went to Simonstown harbour.

The rains were coming. Isaac knew he should be glad, but he was so scared that the murmur of adult voices came, for once, as a relief.

He listened carefully to where they came from and walked in their direction until he came to a clearing where three men in dark grey suits hunched around a pile of wooden crates. The bearded man, with his wide-brimmed cream fedora perched at a dangerous angle on his head, was holding a clear glass bottle filled with a smooth amber liquid.

'The colour's right,' he said. He brought the bottle to his mouth, and — this impressed Isaac! — pulled the cork out with his teeth. He sniffed the open neck and nodded. 'Smells right, too,' he said.

The bearded man sounded nice, thought Isaac. So he left the cover of the bushes and, with a few eager strides, he reached the man. Tugging at his coat, Isaac asked politely, as Ma had taught him, 'Please can I have a drink, Mister? I'm thirsty.'

He was about to add that he was lost, too, but a thunderbolt crackled before he could frame the words.

At first, as he lay in the dirt with his ears ringing and his cheek stinging, Isaac thought the storm had come as suddenly as the veldt rains did. But the two men on the other side of the pile of crates were scrambling to their feet, reaching for weapons Isaac hadn't seen earlier. They were long, ugly, grey things, but still, neither man looked as menacing as the bearded man towering over Isaac, his fist raised and his pearl-grey spats planted firmly apart, as he lay there, helpless and afraid.

But before Isaac could cry out, he heard another sound.

'*Crrt! Crrt!*' his friend the grasshopper said and landed on the bearded man's nose, the sharp little hooks on its legs holding tight even as the man screamed and slapped at his face as he stepped backwards, straight into the open crate. With a loud crash, the crate broke, and the man fell face-first into the other crates.

All Isaac could hear was breaking glass and shouting men and the urgent '*Crrt! Crrt!*' as his hopper flew past him into the bush.

He knew what to do. He scrambled up and, without even a glance in the direction of the flailing

man, ran as fast as he could into the bush the
grasshopper had landed on.

When the noise in the clearing had died, one
of the other men asked, 'Should we find the kid?'

'*Ag* no!' said the bearded man. 'He was too
young. With the storm coming, he'll get lost. By the
time they find him, he'll be dead, or we'll be gone.'

His laugh made Isaac shiver. Only the soft
Crrt! Crrt! at his ear slowed his heartbeat.

He turned towards the sound and saw his old
friend. Gently, he lifted a finger and stroked the
hammer-shaped head, smiling as the antennae tickled
his skin. Looking into those beady orange eyes, he
thought they were remarkably like Ma's eyes when
he'd done something he shouldn't and was in deep
trouble.

So when the creature hopped from bush to
bush slowly, Isaac had no trouble keeping up with it.
He followed it happily, trusting that, like Ma, it knew
what was best for him.

Sure enough, just as the wind blew the last of
the storm clouds away again, with one last bound and
a loud *CRRT!*, the grasshopper burst out of a bush and
landed, a startling splash of colour, on the bonnet of
Oom Japie van Deventer's smart black police car.

Oom Japie was Ma's brother and a *Sersant*.
Isaac flung himself into his uncle's arms and told him
about the bearded man and the bottles of golden
liquid. He could even describe the clearing where
he'd found them. *Oom* Japie swelled with excitement.
'I know which clearing that is,' he growled, plonking
Isaac in his car's front seat. 'Stay there!' he ordered
and called to his men.

It wasn't long before *Oom* Japie was back to
drive Isaac home to where Ma stood under the wide-
spread canopy of the old Nyala tree; the baby hitched
on her hip, her eyes anxiously scanning the bushes
beyond the old rusty fence.

Oom Japie forestalled her scold. 'He's a brave young man, your son,' he said and ruffled Isaac's black curls. 'He found the hideout of that gang of liquor thieves I've been after for months. There's a reward, too,' he added, '£500.'

Isaac didn't know how much £500 was, but Ma's gasp told him it was a lot of money. It was enough, at least, to buy the bicycle he'd wanted. And, although all through the hot, dry days of summer, he often heard his friend the hopper calling and calling, Isaac never again went out into the bush alone.

The Returning
(My Sister, My Sister)

The last I saw of Middletown was The Lights. Dancing over Flamingo Pond, the blue and green and pink orbs bobbed through the air as they had ever since Middletown was built a hundred and eighty-five years ago.

When she took me to see The Lights for the first time, my grandmother — who had heard the story from her grandmother, who'd heard it from *her* grandmother — told me The Lights weren't lights at all but visitors from the wild beyond. The Lights, Ouma said, came from that vast emptiness of the night sky that, with an irresistible promise of better times, beautified the god-forsaken bleakness that surrounded Middletown during the day.

Those colourful bubbles floating through the darkness were magical to my three-year-old eyes. I stared and stared at them, my arm around Ouma's neck as she lifted me.

'For a better view,' she said, but I think it was so she could see my face as I fell in love with those strange, mystery lights that appeared every year in early spring.

No one knew why The Lights came when they did or why they left the first day the wind carried a hint of winter through the streets of Middletown. In the summer, scientists hired every spare room or empty house, tramping off into the falling night as The Lights rose at dusk and tramping wearily back as The Lights disappeared at dawn, leaving them as puzzled as when they arrived.

But Ouma knew, and I knew. The Lights came to visit *us*.

At that first gathering I attended, I hugged Ouma tighter and listened to their babbling chatter, reminding me of the sounds my baby sister had made since she arrived home in Mama's arms.

'You must help me look after her, Tina,' Mama said, smiling, not at me, but at the pink-cheeked wonder wrapped in a soft blanket she held in her arms. 'You're her big sister, and that's what big sisters do.'

I didn't answer, only pressed myself closer to Mama's side, mesmerised by those big blue eyes that, even then, stared right at the secrets I carried.

That night, Ouma took me to meet The Lights. As they gurgled and murmured, echoing a thousand unseen voices, all calling, calling, I never dreamed that when I left Middletown a dozen years later, I wouldn't know who I hated more: my sister or The Lights.

Both betrayed me. My sister's wickedness I'd come to expect, but The Lights — my ancestors, my friends — their betrayal scoured my very soul.

Even before she could speak, Gillian, with her bluebell eyes and blonde hair so white the summer sun turned it translucent, knew how to bend us to her will.

I wasn't quite the slavish fan that Mama and Papa were, or the neighbours, or even the village incomers, those clever scientists who left the city behind for a weekend of mystery lights and magic. All of them — except me and Ouma and The Lights — surrendered to the shimmering blue of her pleading gaze. Whether it was an ice cream cone or a coin pressed into her chubby, eager hand, even strangers could only see her. I ceased to exist except in the hearts of Ouma and The Lights. I was only Tina, Gillian's big sister.

'Let Gillian have it,' Mama would say, not looking at me, never looking at me, her face, usually strained and tired from helping Papa run the office in the garage, shining with happiness as she hovered over Gillian's bed. Papa was the only mechanic in Middletown, so the tiny apartment we lived in above the garage was always filled with papers and spare parts.

'Tigger's my favourite, Mama,' I'd say, hugging the fluffy toy tighter.

'No, he's not,' Mama would say, leaning down and taking the toy away from me to tickle Gillian's tummy as she chortled her charm. 'Barney's your favourite. Gillian likes Tigger.'

As my sister's eyes turned from the murky navy of a newborn into the ice blue they'd remain for the rest of her short life, I shrunk back more and more. There were shadows in those eyes, shadows moving behind the piercing blue, shifting and darkening with an emptiness at odds with the giggles and gurgles she made when she captivated another adult.

Tigger wasn't the last of my possessions that Gillian stole. The older she grew, the more brazen she became. Whenever she wanted anything of mine, she first crawled, then walked across the line dividing our small bedroom.

No matter how much I complained to Mama, she refused to listen.

'She's just a baby, Tina,' Mama would say. 'Have some patience with her.'

I tried to argue that I was only little, too. 'No! No buts!' Mama's finger, with its short stubby nail, would point accusingly at me. 'You're not an only child anymore. You must learn to share; you can't keep everything for yourself.'

Every time Mama refused to listen, Gillian, with her sweet smile and shadowed eyes, pushed me further and further into the loneliness of the least favourite child.

My grandmother — Ouma — would hold me tight, gently pulling my fingers away from my mouth before the nails began to bleed where I bit them, bit them to hold in the muddle of emotions I felt every time Gilliam won another round.

'It's so unfair,' I'd sob into Ouma's warm shoulder, the smell of her old English Lavender powder both comforting and suffocating.

'Hush, child, hush,' she'd murmur, stroking her hand, the knuckles gnarled with age and decades of scrubbing other people's floors. They were the most beautiful hands in the world, for they were the only hands of love I knew after Gillian arrived and stole all of Mama's attention.

Ouma took me to The Lights every night, from their first appearance in spring until their disappearance as autumn set in. Always exhausted from running around keeping Gillian happy, Mama never complained when Ouma said, 'I'm taking Tina for a drive, Mary.'

'Oh, thanks, Ma – that'll help. I can bathe Gilly without worrying about Tina.'

Ouma looked at me in that particular way she had. We both knew Mama only cared about the baby, that wriggling bundle that ruled her with endless smiles and screams.

'When I'm gone,' Ouma said as we sat on the red-and-white-and-black checked blanket she always kept in her car for these nights we shared. 'The Lights will still be here.'

'You live with us, Ouma. Where will you go?'

'I'm an unwanted guest in your mother's home, Tina. Mary only puts up with me because of Josiah.' She pointed to The Lights. 'They're my real home. They're where I'll go when it's my time.' She sighed, squeezing my hand. 'I'm old, Tina, too old to share my son with another woman and in a small apartment.' She wiped at the tears dripping from the corners of her eyes into the wrinkles that criss-crossed her cheeks. 'My time to leave is close, but when I'm gone, you must come and whisper your troubles to me, to The Lights. Even if I don't answer in words, I'll hear you. You'll never be alone, even if you feel everyone only loves Gillian.' She turned a watery smile on me and tapped my nose. 'A secret — that's what it'll be. Our secret.'

My heart overflowed as I hugged her as tight as I could. She knew! She knew everything! And still she loved me!

Soon after Ouma entered The Lights, my secret lay heavier than ever for being unspoken. Gillian would look at me with those ice-blue eyes, that half-smile always chasing away those curious shadows on her face. 'Don't cry, Tina,' she'd say, the deliberate wobble in her voice immediately winning a soothing murmur from Mama.

With Ouma gone, I could only unburden my heart to The Lights. They hovered there, blinking and bubbling, their whispers becoming louder and louder as I told them about each and every battle with Gillian.

As she grew older, she became sneakier and sneakier.

When we went to the Dragonsback Mountains, the vast range of towering mountain peaks rising out of the dusty plains just beyond Middletown's borders, Gillian was seven years to my ten. I wanted to walk to the cave paintings. Ouma had told me how, as a child on her father's sheep farm, her brothers had taken her up into the mountains to the caves of the First People. She'd spoken of how they'd all stripped down, as naked as Adam and Eve in the Garden of Eden, before the wilderness had overwhelmed them and they'd fallen. Ouma and her brothers swam in the crystal clear mountain pool, cooling after the long trek from the farmhouse to the caves. There, they'd touched the ancient red ochre figures, elongated and stick-thin, frozen in a painted dance around a fire. It was there, Ouma said, that she first learned of The Lights, for as the sun had started to sink, the dying rays glancing off the walls, the cave had glittered and murmured with so many lights she'd fainted.

Later, her brothers said she'd dreamed the lights, for none had seen or heard the shimmering radiance that had dazzled her. They'd only seen the stalactites dripping down from the cave ceiling. When she'd whispered of The Lights to her Ouma — my great-great grandmother — she was told that, while The Lights showed themselves to many, they only spoke to the chosen few.

When Mama and Papa said they were taking us into the mountains where Papa's family had lived for generations before bad rains and cattle thieves had pushed them off the land and into Middletown, I wanted to see those caves where The Lights first appeared to Ouma. Of course, Gillian, afraid of what The Lights whispered to me about the secrets hidden behind her eyes, insisted she wanted to see the waterfall that looked like a bride's veil.

'That's such a pretty name, Tina,' she said, her soft, girlish voice cautious. Those guileless blue eyes watched anxiously for my reaction, knowing that Mama and Papa would hear only the sweetness and not her resolve to be the centre of our family.

'The cave walk is too far for you kids,' Papa chimed in. 'There's not enough shade, and the sun is already too high.' He bent and swooped Gillian onto his shoulders like he used to do with me before I was told I was big enough to walk alone. 'We'll take the forest path to the falls and picnic there. It's a steeper route, but the trees make it cooler.'

Having got what she wanted, Gillian squealed
with delight, 'Down, Papa, put me down!'

When he did, she ran and threw her arms
around me. 'You'll love it there, Tina. We can look
for fairies and maybe...' Feeling my tightly held
disappointment, she dropped her arms, and her voice
wobbled as she said, 'Tina doesn't want to see the
bride's veil, Mama.' She stepped back, half behind
Mama's legs, whispering as if afraid of me, 'We
should go to the caves so Tina is happy.'

That was how she did it. That was how she
controlled us all, with that act of sweetness. I almost
doubted myself, but then the sunlight glittered behind
her head, the tips of her hair dancing in the soft
breeze, touched by The Lights that showed me, as
much as Mama's voice did, that she wasn't what she
seemed.

'Tina must learn that she can't always have
what she wants in life,' Mama said.

'But I want Tina to be happy, Mama,' Gillian
said pathetically. Mama's tight-lipped look faded
instantly into a warm look of approval as her hand
dropped down to cup Gillian's head in a gentle stroke.
'You're a poppet for always trying to please your
sister, Gilly. Tina doesn't know how lucky she is to
have a sister like you.'

I could have wept out of loneliness then, out
of the depths of a ten-year-old child's frustration and
pain at being both misunderstood and excluded from
the love that had once been mine and mine alone
before Gillian came along.

That day — a day that should have been filled
with the unblemished happiness of childhood — only
got worse.

As we walked through the forest in our usual
order — Papa, Gillian, me, then Mama — the path,
snaking close to the edge of the mountain, curved
around a dead old yellowwood, the roots gnarled and

twisting across the path so that I tripped and fell into Gillian, the palms of my hands hitting her, accidentally, in the middle of her back just as she was easing herself along the narrowing path around the tree.

She screamed and screamed all the way down the mountain, just as Mama and Papa screamed and screamed as we stood and watched her body bounce from rock to rock until it landed, silent and still, on a ledge, except for the golden hair, blowing in the slight breeze that tangled it in the stunted protea that had stopped her fall.

Mama refused to believe me when I said it was an accident. Papa believed me, but he was too wrapped up in grieving Gillian to see that Mama, far from loving me again as she had before Gillian arrived, could barely speak to me or touch me.

There was no one to listen to me — except The Lights. The Lights were my only friends all the rest of that summer and the five summers before I left Middletown. I would talk to them and hear Ouma's voice whispering in the darkness, her voice muted by the rustling leaves of the trees surrounding Flamingo Park.

'Tell the truth, Tina. Tell your Mama about Gillian. When she knows, she'll love you again, as she did before, and everything will be wonderful again.'

One day, I told Mama. I told her the truth about Gillian, about the shadow of evil hiding in the back of her eyes, and how she stole everything from me, even Mama's love.

'You're the evil one,' Mama screamed. 'You're like that crazy Ouma of yours. Her jealousy of Josiah's love — my *husband's* love! — made my life a living hell! Now you! *You* were jealous of Gillian!'

'I wasn't, Mama. I wasn't! It was Gillian!'

Sobbing, I tried to put my arms around Mama. Screwing her face up, she shoved me away. 'Don't touch me,' she said, backing towards the stairs. 'I can't stand you touching me!'

'Mama...'

'I want Gillian! I want my baby back!'

I knew then, even from the grave, Gillian had won.

And The Lights had betrayed me. They had lied when they said Mama would love me again.

Cold, far colder than the autumn breeze that blew The Lights away every year, I said, 'You hate me.'

I understood now that The Lights must have known that truth even as they urged me to tell my secret to Mama, to tell Mama how evil Gillian had been.

My face was wet with tears. Wiping the dribble of snot from my top lip, I started towards where Mama, fingers tightly gripping the steel railing that wound up the stairs, stood beneath a giant photograph of Gillian. Immortalised on canvas soon after she fell down the mountain, her ice-blue eyes and blonde hair dominated the landing as she had dominated everything in my world from the moment Mama arrived home from the hospital with her wrapped in that pale pink blanket.

'Stay away from me,' Mama cried, 'Stay away...!'

The police said even though I was only fifteen years old then, I had criminal capacity. No one, not even Papa this time, believed me when I said it was an accident. All I had wanted to do was throw the painting of Gillian down the stairs. Remove it so that her evil shadow no longer darkened our lives. Mama's fall down the stairs was an accident, a terrible accident, just like that sunshine day in the Dragonsback Mountains when Gillian had fallen down the mountain to her death.

As they took me away after the trial, the last I saw of Middletown was The Lights. Dancing over Flamingo Pond, the blue and green and pink orbs bobbed through the air.

'Sharp-sharp, brah,' I said to the Cape Town taxi driver who, one summer evening fifteen years later, dropped me off on the outskirts of Middletown on his way to Johannesburg. Still sleepy, still small and tired, Middletown hadn't changed. The Lights were there, too, still bobbing in the dusk over Flamingo Pond.

I shrugged my backpack onto my shoulder, the khaki canvas faded with age and stained with, well, I wasn't sure what but, as I'd picked it up from a trolley bin outside the Blue Route Mall soon after they'd released me from Pollsmoor, I didn't complain.

Papa still lived in our apartment over the garage on Riverside Avenue. Papa, who had loved me even after Gillian had died and who, after Mama died and I went away, still sent money once a year on my birthday.

I couldn't help the quickening of my breath, the heavy beat of my heart.

Papa would love me still, I knew. Of course, he would.

I started the short walk home, and The Lights winked and bobbed in agreement.

The Blue Mountains

The day I left my childhood behind, I played in the mud on the edge of a field of fading yellow sunflowers. The shadows of the mountains fell over me as my mother, her still-pretty face tense with worry, ran up to me. My father, his narrow forehead decorated in the elaborate blue-and-white beaded band that told of his chiefdom, followed more sedately.

'Wife,' he said, resting a hand on my mother's shoulder. The nail of his right forefinger twisted crookedly from the time when, as a child my age, he'd struggled to free a lost calf. A rock, loose and heavy in the red soil that covered so much of the barren heights of the Blue Mountains, fell and crushed his finger, forever marking the nail. 'You knew when you married me this time would come.'

My mother, her hands twisting into her stomach as if that way she could stop her wrenching tears, only wailed. 'She's just a baby!'

'Chiamaka is six years old. No younger than I was.'

'But she's a *girl*!' Another wail escaped her, this one so deep her breasts, still sumptuous after suckling seven children, jiggled. 'You have your sons.'

'The law of the ancestors says, "*all the chief's children.*"' My father's face was tight; he loved her so much that he had only taken one wife. His reward was the seven children my mother bore him, all healthy and all living. I was the youngest and the only daughter. He didn't want to hurt her, but his dark gaze was implacable as it rested on me, naked but for the

red ooze of mud clinging to my skin as I sat in the
puddle that was to become the final playground of my
childhood.

'She should learn how to grind the corn and
make *iPhutu pap*. She should learn to braid hair and
care for children … don't you want grandchildren?'
Her emotion overwhelming her, my mother—for the
first time in my life—dropped to her knees, as she
should do when supplicating a chief such as my
father. Although it was his right, as Chief of the
Luvenda, he, in his wisdom and his love, had never
demanded this usual sign of submission from her.

'Stop your wailing, wife.' He shook her hands
free from their hold on the strip of leopard skin that
crossed under his chin, across the lean planes of his
chest until it tucked into his loincloth decorated with
the same blue-and-white symbols as his headband.
'Chiamaka may not be The One.' His voice was stern
enough to silence my mother, but with her head
lowered to the sand, she could not see what I saw: the
glitter of moisture adding a sheen to his brown eyes
that turned them as blue as the distant mountains.

I knew then that he knew I *was* The One. In
the heavy swirl of excitement that engulfed me, I
started to hiccup, and with each *hic*, I felt myself
growing a little taller as I stood up from the mud
puddle and waited for my destiny.

'Come, daughter,' my father said, holding out
his broad hand, with its strong spatula fingers that
always made me feel so safe. 'This time, you will
come to the *khoro*. Your brothers are already
waiting.'

My hiccups stopped: born ten years after the
youngest of my father's six sons and a girl, I wasn't
close to any of them, for they saw me as a child. But
being included in the village council meeting must
mean I was fully grown. I stood up, ineffectually
wiping the mud from my body until my mother, silent

still since my father's order, plucked some green sunflower leaves and, with a few strategic wipes, had me as clean as I could ever be without immersing myself in the river that watered our land.

Soon, we arrived at the ancient baobab tree, where my brothers and all the people of the village milled around its massive trunk as they waited for the *khoro* to begin. Red dust puffed around the hundreds of bare feet tramping the hallowed ground, made smooth as a river-washed stone by the many gatherings before this one. This tree, the legends said, had stood for ten thousand years, providing our people with food, medicine, and shelter.

Despite the lowing of a large herd of cattle held back by a few roughly stripped acacia tree branches, there was an unearthly silence hanging over the waiting people: the silence of breath held as one waited for the assegai to fly from the hand of a warrior. Only the occasional squawk of a baby—disturbed from its slumber as its mother dropped to her knees before the Chief, my father, walking past her on the path opening through the crowd—broke the still air.

In front of the gnarled old trunk stood my brothers, from the eldest at nearly thirty summers to the youngest, but ten years older than I, murmuring to the *Makhadzi*, the old woman who, when our people were sick, spoke to our ancestors to heal our spirits and gave us herbs to heal our bodies.

As was customary, my mother stopped as we reached the edge of the low-hanging branches, spreading out from the heavy trunk like the arms of a mother protecting her family. I held her hand tightly, too scared to tell her to stop crying, that the patter of excitement running through my veins as softly as a mouse ran through the grass roof of our hut in the shadows of the night was nothing to cry about.

Realising I was no longer at his side, my father turned to me. 'Come, Chia,' he said, and the sadness was back in his eyes, but pride was there too, and a quiet encouragement.

'She can't come into the circle,' my third oldest brother snarled. 'She's a girl!' My other brothers, brave now another had spoken, grumbled their agreement.

'Chia is here for the same reason you are,' my father said, 'because I have called for her presence.'

My brother dropped his gaze first.

Then the *Makhadzi*, her rough cloth skirt woven in the colours of the autumn trees and swirling in a gust of hot wind, stepped forward, raising the bent wooden stick she carried to the sky.

'The time is now,' she said. In descending height, she lined up all seven of my father's children beside him. She handed him his cow-skin shield and assegai and threw his leopard-skin cloak around his shoulders, attaching a crown of antelope skin to his beaded headband, with two large ostrich feathers that bobbed and weaved with each movement he made.

She scraped twigs and dried branches together and set them alight. She began chanting, at first softly, then louder and louder as the twigs smouldered, and when the first flame leapt from the crackling mound, she scattered herbs into the fire: rosemary for clarity and the sacred *imphepo* herb to call to the spirits of our ancestors.

The smell and the smoke made my head spin, and my heart beat faster and faster as she started beating her drum in time with her chants until my father held up his assegai, and she abruptly fell silent.

As the smoke of the sacred herbs swirled in the silence around us, my father began to speak.

'My people, one day I will no longer be Chief.' Cries broke from the villagers' throats, for he was a much-loved leader, but he stilled them by holding up his assegai. 'The way of nature is that from the Earth we have come, and to her, we all must return.'

He dropped the point of his spear to the ground, flicking up a scattering of dust that fell from its tip, glinting in the sun, as he continued, 'The laws of the tribe and of the tribal ancestors will choose my successor as your Chief.'

'When my ancestors came to me in the night, visiting my dreams and whispering into my heart, they told me the time had come to begin training the next leader of our people.' He pointed at his cattle, unsettled and restless from the chanting and the smoke, and said, 'I will divide my cattle into seven herds: you, my children, will each care for a herd for one full cycle of the moon. You will take food and, two days hence, when the moon is full and pale, you will each drive your herd into the foothills of the Blue Mountains.'

His first son, my oldest brother, would go toward the Dragon's Back, he said; his second son towards the Dragon's Spear and so on, until he came to me.

'And you, Chia, will take the seventh herd into the Valley of the Pregnant Woman.'

My brothers shuffled and shifted with unease and looked at me, then at each other, with sullen eyes, but no one, not even Kofi, my third-oldest brother and the strongest, dared interrupt him.

'My successor as Chief of the Luvenda people will be chosen by this method,' he continued. 'You will each care for your herd, and when the moon has gorged the sky empty of stars and is full of light again, you will bring my cattle back to me.'

He looked us over, one by one. '*All* of my cattle,' he said, 'For if you cannot look after the beasts in the field, how can you look after your people?'

As we left the village, my excitement was as sharp as my fear. This was the most responsibility I'd ever had: were my brothers' whispers true?

'A girl has no place in the line of Chiefs!' Kofi had complained.

'Let him give her a herd; she's only a girl,' they laughed. I'd glared at them, but they only laughed again. 'She's too young and, surely, as the sun rises each morning, she'll kill all the cattle—or herself—long before the stars disappear into the belly of the moon again.'

My father had insisted, so I, too, left with my bundle of food. With more running than I had ever done before and using the same crooning noises my mother had sung to calm me as a baby when the fierce storms raged over the kraals, I drove the unruly cattle ahead of me with a stick.

The days that followed were hard and hot, and the nights cold and long, but I learnt how to calm the animals when the growl of a hungry leopard echoed across the valley hidden beneath the towering mountains. I learned how to care for them as if they were the children I would one day have, and I even learned how to birth a new calf, for within the first few days, I realised one of the cows was pregnant.

When her time came, in the middle of one of the storms I dreaded so much, she lowed and lowed with pain. Praying to the ancestors of my people for help and, as I'd seen the *Makhadzi* do from time to time with the wailing women of the village, I pushed my hand up the cow's tunnel of life and, cupping the calf's nose, gently twisted it around until it slipped into the world in a watery rush.

The following day, it was gone from the small kraal I'd built from scraps of wood I'd found near the cave I was sleeping in. After hours of searching, of following its bawls, I found it in an underground cave, sparkling with the tears of the gods that had dripped through the earth above and settled into the darkness of the pool below where my lost calf calmly stood drinking its fill. Its soft brown coat glistened in the light, bouncing off the glittering rocks as the sun, rising to its peak, shone into the cave through a slender crack. I whirled round and round until exhausted from my exhilaration. Falling on my knees next to the calf, I drank gratefully from the pool before leading it back to the herd, caged in the rough kraal I had made.

By the time the moon was full again, I knew each of the cattle by the different markings on their coats, and each had a name.

I was disinclined to rush back to the village and become a mere girl again, playing in the mud pools or helping grind the corn, but eventually, I arrived back in the village, driving my herd ahead of me.

My mother was wailing; my father pacing, and Kofi, his third son, gloating: until my arrival, he was the only one who had returned with the same number of cattle as he'd had when he left.

'You're back,' my father said. He gave a slight cough, clearing his throat as he gripped my shoulder hard, even as my mother fell on her knees, examining every part of me for injury or harm.

'Of course,' I said as I shrugged off my mother's attentions, for she was fussing over the child I no longer was.

His laugh boomed like a crack of thunder, and his grip tightened for an instant before he turned to count the cattle I had herded into the village. He counted the last head and turned to look at me.

'You're a good girl,' he praised, 'and you'll make a fine Chief on the day I return to the fields of our ancestors.'

Chaos erupted.

'*I'm* your successor!' Kofi said, balling his hand so tightly the skin looked thin and smooth. 'I am your son! I am older than Chia!' With each sentence, he banged his fist into his chest and shook it at his herd. 'And I, too, brought back all my cattle!'

The Chief, our father, was unmoved. 'So you did,' he said. 'Didn't you?' He pointed his flywhisk at my brother's herd, and the snail shells and black feathers of the fish eagle on its handle twirled slyly. 'Do you know their names yet?'

'Names? What names?' Kofi frowned. 'Cattle don't have names.'

My father turned to me. 'Chiamaka, do *your* cattle have names?'

I nodded.

'What is the calf called?' He pointed to the young calf I had helped birth. She'd become my favourite, and as I rubbed her silky head, she mooed and tried to lick me.

'Glittering Tear.'

As my brothers, led by my third brother Kofi, guffawed, my father ignored them. A smile touched his lips, such a small smile I couldn't even see the missing tooth at the back of his mouth, which only showed when he laughed loudly. He nodded. 'Where did you get her name?'

I dropped my chin, avoiding his eyes, for I realised I'd have to tell him how close I'd come to losing one of my herd. 'Come, child.' I shivered as the coarse horsetail of his flywhisk scratched my chin as he used it to lift my gaze to his. 'Tell us how you found that name.'

My voice faltering at times so that he had to ask me to repeat myself, I told how I'd almost lost the calf, not once, at her birth, but twice, when she escaped to the cave of the glittering tears.

But, 'That is a good name, Chia,' was all he said when I finished my tale. Then he asked me, 'Have you named every one of these beasts that depend on you? Even the oldest? The weakest?'

'I know every name of every beast in my herd,' I said, my chin tilting up, even though I knew I should not be so proud of such a simple task. 'That one is Granny because she is so old,' I said, 'and that brown one, with the white patch, is White Eye and—'

His full lips held onto his smile, and his eyes half-closed as he interrupted me to ask my brother, 'Do you see, Kofi? Chia even named the old cattle, while you could not name one of the animals in your herd.'

'I was too busy to give the dumb animals names,' sneered my brother as he wiped away sweat rolling down his cheek, even though the sun was starting to slide behind the *khoro* tree, bringing welcome relief from the heat.

My father's flywhisk stopped its steady *whishwhishwhish*. 'Come here,' he ordered.

Kofi sauntered up to us, his loincloth hitched low under his belly fat, swirling around his knees, and the rattles attached to the strips of impala pelts around his ankles jingling with each confident step.

My father held up his finger, the one crushed long ago, and said, 'Tell me again, third son of mine, why, when the sun sets on this day, you should be named my successor as Chief?'

'I am a man.' He thumped his bare chest, already thick with fat. The village knew Kofi liked more than his share when we gathered to eat together in the shade of the *boma*. 'I am older than Chia.'

Encouraged by the rising mutters of the listening villagers, he continued, 'And, while my first brother lost ten cattle and my fourth brother lost his whole herd, I—' he paused triumphantly, his bare feet spread wide apart in the dust to balance his weight as his chest swelled out like an old brown river toad calling to its mate, '—I brought back every beast I left with.'

'*All* your herd?' my father asked, that slight smile still tugging at the corner of his mouth. 'Did you really?'

'Did I what?'

'Bring back every beast you left with?'

'Yes!'

My father said nothing, and all the villagers fell silent until the only noise was the flywhisk moving back and forth, back and forth, with the occasional dart and slap that killed an errant fly with deceptive ease.

Kofi glared at me, then at my father. 'Except for the calf!' he shouted. 'One of the cows was pregnant! She gave birth to a girl calf, but it wandered off, and I couldn't find it. It bawled for days,' he snarled. 'But I couldn't find it.'

'And yet Chia—she who is the youngest of you all, and a girl, and for these reasons you say she is unworthy to be Chief—she found her calf and brought it back safely with all the rest of her herd.'

He stood up and called the *Makhadzi*. Together, they came and stood with me, one on either side.

'My people,' my father said. 'Never before has it come to pass that our people have had a woman as Chief. But the gods and the ancestors have spoken! One day, when I return to the dust of this land, which has sustained our forefathers for generations, Chiamaka will be your Chief.'

The crowd hissed and muttered, but he ignored them. 'She will be your light and your leader, and you will honour her as you honour me.' He pulled himself taller and glared the rising noise into silence. 'Or the mountains will no longer thunder, the river will dry up, and our people will become strangers to each other.'

For a long time, no one moved. Afraid of the silence, which made the air feel like the moments before the storms that rolled off the mountains and thundered around us, I scrabbled for my father's hand. He did not say a word, and the silence grew until my mother dropped to her knees.

'The gods have spoken,' she cried. 'Chiamaka will be Chief.'

Slowly, then in greater numbers, the crowd fell to their knees until only my brothers stood before us. Still, my father did not speak, and as I looked up at his face, I saw from the muscles clenching along his jaw that his quietness was not that of calm but of a strong man mastering his anger so that it did not tear asunder that which he loved the most: his people.

Whishwhishwhish went his flywhisk until, on almost a sigh, they gave up their struggle against his greater strength and, one by one, with Kofi last to surrender, they sank to their knees to acknowledge the line of chiefs that was to endure through me.

That same night, the *Makhadzi* took me high into the Blue Mountains to learn the ways of Chief of the Luvenda, leaving her great niece to take her place as soothsayer of the village.

We passed the muddy sunflower field where I had said goodbye to my childhood; we walked through the green foothills, up into the dense sacred forests of tree ferns and fever trees, and then crossed into the barrenness of the snow-capped mountaintops.

There were stretches of grey slate, with a few stubby bushes to break the dullness. As we trudged on and on, the air became thin and cold, even in the heat of summer. Between my gasps for breath, I pointed to a few stubborn patches of snow.

'That snow is the gift of our ancestors,' said
the old woman, who was hardly puffing after the long
climb with our supplies. 'It keeps the rivers in the
valley trickling even in the worst droughts, just
enough to save our people.'

A gnarled hand on my arm stopped me.
'Look,' the Makhadzi said, pointing downwards with
her knobkerrie, the tip of the gnarled wooden stick
rubbed smooth and round by her hand.

Far below was the village. Tiny round huts,
with their roofs of grass and walls of mud, scattered
inside the stone walls; people like ants scurrying
around; and the White River that had run through the
centre of the village for as long as my people had
existed.

'We have not known drought for generations,
not since your grandfather's grandfather took the
throne,' the old woman said. 'Your lineage is a noble
one. Can you learn what that means?'

A stern thread wove through her voice; when I
looked up into that wrinkled face, her eyes were as
old as the mountains. Something moved inside me,
waking me to seek an answer.

As tired as I was, I pulled myself straighter,
drawing on the strength my father wanted me to have.
'I will learn,' I promised.

Her eyes, small as brown berries dried out
from being in the sun too long, became smaller as she
smiled and walked on until, where the narrow path
that led us up the mountain became almost impossible
to pass, we turned a corner and found an old hut.

The stone walls stood firm, although they bore
the scars of the fire that had destroyed the roof and
blackened the door and walls.

'What happened?' I asked.

'The finger of the gods,' the old woman said,
'knows the right time to strike.' As if hearing her, far

in the belly of the mountains, there was a faint flash, followed by the rumble of thunder.

I shivered and asked, 'Who lives here?'

'The future Chiefs of our people live here,' she said and dropped her heavy sack to the ground, stretching as far as her bent old bones would allow. 'We will live here. Fetch those stones.' She pointed to the pieces of slate piled beneath a jagged ledge. 'We begin again.'

Half frozen with cold, for the day had begun to slip into the shadows of the night, and half frozen with fear of the future, I rubbed my hands together to stop their shaking. '*Makhadzi*, how long are we to rest here?'

'Until you are ready to lead your people.'

'How long will that take?'

'Questions, child, so many questions!' She sighed and answered me anyway. 'The mountains will tell us when you are ready.'

Only my stomach growled in reply. Ashamed, hoping the old woman hadn't heard the sound, I looked around at the land, which looked even more unfriendly as the night began to swallow it up, and I whispered, 'What if our supplies run out? How will we eat?'

'What your father does not leave underneath the Baboon Rock each full moon, the mountains will provide.'

So it was.

The rains came, and the rains went for many seasons. Even as my body changed from a girl's into a woman's, the mountains taught me what the *Makhadzi* did not. I grew used to the crack of thunder and the flash of light that told us the gods were still pleased with our people.

I watched the grounds for signs of drought.

'As chief, you must bring the rains to both the land and the spirits of the people,' the *Makhadzi* said. 'When the land is dusty and dry, our people are starving their souls, so the ancestors starve their bellies to make them remember. You must make them remember, even if it is painful.'

I scanned the horizon for the changing colours and the flights of the birds, all clues as to when the rain would come rolling off the mountains.

'Remember what?' I asked, looking down at her, for as I had become taller, she had shrunk with age.

'Remember the source of their abundance.' She leaned a little heavier on her stick and sighed. 'Too often, the people only remember the gods in times of drought.' She smiled sadly, her head, with its thin grey hair nearly white now, bobbing up and down. 'In times when the corn is plenty, and the animals are fat, they forget too easily. That's when you will need to call down the power of the gods. Come,' she said, 'I will show you how to make the mountains cry the tears of the gods.'

But I never could learn how to make rain roll off the mountains into the valley below as she did. Soon, she was too old to make the heavens weep, and the lands got drier and drier.

One morning, after the moon had hung full and heavy in the dark sky, so close to the earth I could have touched it had I been taller, I woke to find her curled, still and serene. Her cow skin was wrapped tightly around her, and all I had to do through my tears was scratch a shallow grave beneath the cold grey shale surrounding our hut.

Before the next full moon, I walked halfway down the mountain and waited at the Baboon Rock for the one who brought our supplies from the village.

'The *Makhadzi* is dead,' I said when the son of my brother's wife's uncle arrived. 'Tell my father I am ready to return to the village.'

At the next full moon, the answer was the same as it was for another hundred moons:

'The Chief says you still have much to learn and must not come home.'

He was right. I still had much to learn.

The mountains grew silent and dry as I struggled to learn how to make the rains come.

Even the snows of the winters were thinner, their melt sinking through the cracks in the blue slate peaks long before the water could gorge the river in the valley that had saved our people for generations.

One moon, when I went to Baboon Rock, there were no supplies, not then and not for two more full moons. I dared not leave the mountain until my father gave his permission. I survived by eating the tadpoles, breeding in the muddy pools trapped between the cracks and crevices. Occasionally, I caught a frog or a lizard, but I grew weaker and scared until the only thunder I heard was that of my rumbling stomach.

It was a cold night, too late for the rains when my father came to me.

'Chiamaka,' he said. 'Return to the village of the Luvenda. Return to your home.'

Although it had been years since I heard him speak, the lilt of his voice was no different from when, as a young girl, I played in the sunflower field, the stroke of his calloused hand on my cheek as gentle as ever.

'I'm not ready,' I cried. 'I cannot make the mountains weep.'

'You must return,' he said, withdrawing his hand from my cheek, but when I clutched at his fingers to hold him close, I woke, crying.

In the morning, I gathered my few belongings. The old *Makhadzi*'s knobkerrie, unused since she had last tried to teach me how to make rain, lay on the floor in the hut. I picked it up, thinking it would help me keep my footing as I descended the steeper parts of the mountains. Besides, when I held it, I could hear the echo of her voice teaching me the sacred rain chants.

Delaying the moment of my departure, for, truly, I was not ready to leave this place, I playfully shook the stick at the heavens.

With swift ferocity, the mountains answered me. A jagged bolt of lightning flew from the sky, setting ablaze the hut that had been my home for more moons than I cared to remember until only the stone walls still stood, as scorched and scarred as when first I had seen them.

The hut was gone, but I still had the old woman's rain stick. I could no longer delay, so my slow trek out of the mountains began. As I passed Baboon Rock, my fear bubbled over into excitement.

In my dreams, my father had not changed.

In life, would he be bent and grey? Would my mother still be pretty? Who of the friends of my youth had married or had children of their own?

But, as I descended from the desolate peaks, my fear returned. For, instead of lush forests and fields of ripe maize and yellow sunflowers, the closer I came to the village, the more desolate the land became.

In the village, people lay drooped across the doorways of their huts or leaned lethargically against trees shrivelled by drought and on the edge of dying. Starving dogs, their ribs showing through matted hair, did no more than bare their teeth at me. After so many years away, I was a stranger in my own village.

'*Aa!*' I greeted the people, old and young, but at the hunger and hopelessness in their faces, I could not add a smile to my greeting.

What had my father done to so anger the gods and bring this terrible drought on them?

Or was it I who had failed my people with my inability to bring the rain as the old *Makhadzi* had tried to teach me?

The sound of shouting, interspersed with a pleading voice I recognised as my mother's, drew me, stumbling, down the path to the *khoro* tree. My mother was on her knees, hands stretched palms upward, her head bowed before the Chief.

But the Chief was not my father…it was Kofi. Dressed in the leopard pelt and blue-beaded headband of the Chief of the Luvenda people, he pushed past my mother to where two of my other brothers held Demba, the last but one of my father's children.

With a vicious swipe, Kofi struck my father's flywhisk across Demba's face and shoulders with such force my mother jumped to her feet to scurry around the edge of them, alternately wringing her hands and covering her face as she cried out for her sons to stop their squabbles.

'I am your Chief.' Kofi screeched, his spittle mixing with the blood on Demba's face. 'You will obey me. Chia stays where she belongs … in the wastes of the accursed Blue Mountains!'

'The wasteland is here, brother. *Here!*' Demba coughed a bubble of blood past his swollen lips. 'You angered the gods when you refused to obey their natural laws—' He broke off as Kofi hit him again, then he continued, his voice weaker but still determined, 'Chia must be called home. She is the rightful Chief.'

'I am Chief!' *Whish!* The flywhisk sliced across Demba's face again, his brown skin stripping white and then pinking into a deep red as the blood

flowed from his wounds. 'You will obey *me*!' *Whish!*
'Not the gods we cannot see and who desert us in our
hour of need!' *Whish!*

Demba's head dropped forward, and my other
brothers let him fall to the ground. My mother, the
thin silver bracelets she wore around her ankles
shivering with her long keening cry, dropped to his
side to wipe the blood away from his closed eyes to
drip instead into the dry dust beneath his head.

Whish! Kofi hit him again, narrowly missing
my mother's hand. '*I* am your Chief!' he snarled.
'Remember that. Chia is dead by now and will never
be Chief.'

'I am not dead,' I said. 'I am here.'

A silence greater than the silence that fell in
the nights high in the mountains descended on the
people gathered under the *khoro* tree. Dropping the
small sack of my belongings to the ground, I knelt
next to my mother at Demba's side. His eyelids
flickered open at the touch of my fingers to his neck.
'Chiamaka!' As his eyes drifted shut again, his breath
settled into a shallow but steady rhythm as he
whispered, 'My Chief!'

I knelt there, at his side, my head bowed low
to hear him speak, my small woman's fist gripping
the knobkerrie of the old *Makhadzi.* At his words, I
felt a weight settle on my shoulders. As light as the
breath of my noble ancestors and as heavy as the
leopard pelt that proclaimed the position of Chief, it
was the knowledge that I had waited too long to
return from the mountains.

Slowly, to give my wobbly knees time to get
used to the new weight they carried, I stood and faced
my brother who wore the Chief's regalia. Stretching
out the knobkerrie, I gently lifted the edge of the
leopard pelt stretching across his fat belly. Now
grown as tall as he, I was also lean and strong from

my years of scavenging in the high, grey wastes that
loomed over the valley.

'Where is my father?' I asked and tapped that
bulging belly of his with the knobkerrie. 'Where is
our Chief?'

With a howl, he grabbed the rain stick from
me and snapped it across his knee.

'He is dead,' he screamed. 'Dead and buried
these last ten years!'

'He cannot be dead,' I whispered, shaken by
the loss of my rain stick and the news I had already
known deep in my heart. 'He came to me last night
and told me to return to the village.'

A collective gasp flew up from the small
crowd, and the wind swept it up, carrying it through
the dying, dusty streets of the village until soon, even
the oldest and the youngest of our people were
clustering around the *khoro* tree, all murmuring and
babbling.

'Chiamaka is here!'

'She is alive.'

'Chiamaka, the Chief, has returned to save us.'

Save them? How could I save them from the
desolation that had greeted my return when, without
my rain stick, I could not even save myself? I could
not make rain; I had never yet been able to make the
Blue Mountains thunder and weep so that the ground
grew thick with crops and the river ran strong with
water.

'STOP!' roared Kofi. '*I* am your Chief!'

'You are no Chief,' I said, 'if your people are
starving while you are fat and well-fed.'

'You are an imposter!' he sneered, throwing
the broken knobkerrie at my feet. 'Where are the rains
that you are supposed to bring?'

I remembered all the times I had been unable
to make the rains come, no matter what the *Makhadzi*
taught me. I looked at her broken stick lying in the

dust at my feet. And I doubted as he did, for I had never yet brought the rains to this land.

I looked at the people before me. Gaunt, starving faces stared at me with the same velvet brown eyes of the calf I had once saved in the cave of the glistening tears. In the distance, I heard the Blue Mountains give a faint rumble, and a lone calf moaned its fear at the unfamiliar sound.

'The rains are coming,' I promised and walked to where the sack of my belongings lay. 'The lands will be watered and the people fed before the sun sets this day.'

With only the sound of the calf lowing in my head and with an assurance I didn't feel, I withdrew what I needed from my sack. A porcupine quill to replace the rain stick; some *imphepo* to burn so that the sacred herb smoke could call to my father and to my father's father for help; and the cracked stone I had found the day I had dug the grave for the old *Makhadzi*.

Ignoring Kofi's shouts as he ordered the villagers to leave, to return to their huts, I began to chant slowly as I packed the wild sage tightly into the fissure with the quill. To some watching, those too young to remember, it was curiosity that kept them in place; to others, the old ones, the ancient rituals I was preparing reminded them of an age gone by when the world had been safer and food more plentiful.

My chanting got louder and louder as the mountains flashed and thundered in reply, and the people and the village faded from my sight in the clouds of smoke. I flew high into the storm clouds and asked for the help of the gods; I begged their forgiveness: we, their people, had strayed from the path of the good spirits. In return for their mercy, I promised them a pure heart. Soon, the gods began to weep.

With a crack that shook wide the gates of heaven, just as I could faintly, oh-so-faintly, see my father and the old *Makhadzi* in the distance, a spear of lightning dropped me to the earth again where I lay with the smell of fire in my nostrils and my face pressed into the dust as it turned to rivulets of mud.

The sound of my people jeering and laughing forced me to push myself to my knees. Little blue flames still leapt along the blackened branches of the smouldering *khoro* tree, licking their way around Kofi's crumpled body, which jerked as the first stone was thrown.

'Imposter!' shouted an unknown voice.

'Thief!' cried another, and he mewled as more stones pelted his bare skin, stripped of the leopard skin that someone had thrown across my shoulders as I had lain exhausted from the rain-making.

'Enough,' I said, for their relief was turning to anger, and that, in turn, would anger the ancestors. Still kneeling in the dirt, I scrabbled closer to Kofi and removed my father's flywhisk from his loosened grasp. Before, when I'd touched it as a child, it had always felt too large for my hand, but today, it felt light and easy in my grasp. Flicking it so it made a gentle *whishwhish*whish through the air, I repeated my command, 'Enough!'

One by one, the hands holding stones opened, the sharp, rough stones dropping to the earth as the people fell to their knees before their Chief, I, Chiamaka.

After that day, Kofi was not the same: docile and obedient, he never uttered another word. He only sat, growing older, staring at the world with the wide eyes of a child who had seen things he'd never thought to see.

Like the dry land, the ancient baobab tree took years to recover from the damage. But, when I was old and grey and called my children to me the day I split my cattle amongst them, the tree, like the land, was rich and greenly abundant again.

A new trunk had grown, covering the scar of the burn with thick new growth. Not hiding it, no, for the past could never be hidden, but embracing it with new hope and new dreams so that both past and present formed one unified trunk that continued to shelter our people as we lived on in the shadows of the great Blue Mountains that had seen an eternity and stood ready to face another.

The Shining of Light

There comes a time, a solitary time — perhaps even a lonely time — in a man's existence. If he's lucky, that time comes but once, and the journey ends after the mountain's snowy peaks have been breached.

For me, though, the journey begins again and again. Sometimes, I am The Seeker of Wisdom. Other times, I shine the light for others who seek the Path of Truth.

As a young man, I lived a life of luxury. Swathed in rich red robes and golden slippers, I drank from golden cups. Quick to lust and quick to anger, there came the day that I killed my brother over a woman.

For a twelve month, I languished in the prison of my own making. My pain filled my world with darkness until The High Priestess, my mother, gifted me with a six-pointed star and a robust wooden staff.

'Go forth into the darkness, my son,' she said, 'and find the gate of the way.'

'What way?' I cried.

'The way of the Light,' she replied.

'How will I know when I find it?'

'Trust in the gods.' She leaned forward from her throne between the pillars of Boaz and Jakin to touch my wet cheek with a gentle finger. 'Listen when their whispers brush your soul with wisdom.'

I went forth into the night, dressed in grey robes and grey slippers. I journeyed through the wilderness until my hair turned white and my beard grew long. For aeons, I travelled the way of sorrow and pain, shunning village and croft. Alone, always alone, except for the whispers within my soul.

As I stumbled across arid deserts in foreign lands and up infinite rocky mountain paths, I gained strength from my wooden staff. When the night was darkest, my lantern guided me along ways unknown until, as the snow melted in the warmth of a new dawn, I left the mountain peak and returned to the place of my birth.

With my sins forgiven and my penance paid, my mother's people gathered around me to hear the tale of the Light Journey.

Some—the brave, the foolish—now look to me to guide them as they traverse their own mountain peaks. I travel ahead, still alone, shining the light for them to follow—or not.

There are still times, though, when the inner darkness devours me anew. It is then I wrap my bowed shoulders in the old grey cloak. I lift my star lantern and my solid wooden staff, and with the uncertain steps of a novice, my solitary quest resumes.

Girl Wonder

If there was one certainty about that dusty dorp in the Free State where Johanna Venter grew up, it was this: boys grew into men, and girls grew into women.

Except, much to Johanna's mother's shame — and hers too — Johanna was born both girl and boy.

'Look, Johanna,' Pa would say. 'Here's another one.' He'd pin a cut-out clownfish on her bedroom wall, carefully lining it up alongside the photos of earthworms and banana slugs above the glass tank housing the giant African land snail he'd bought Johanna as a pet five years ago to show her she wasn't alone in her differentness.

'She's not an animal, Johan!' Ma would say. 'She's supposed to be a *girl*!' She'd dress Johanna in pink frilly dresses with dainty white patent leather sandals that pinched Johanna's broad feet, even as the frills added bulk to her flat-chested, muscular body. She decorated Johanna's bedroom with pink floral curtains and delicate white furniture as if the overdose of pink would somehow make up for the tiny penis she had discovered in her baby girl.

Johanna would glower, her heavy eyebrows lowering every time Ma added to the pink collection. She was all girl in her heart, but at the first opportunity, she'd exchange the frills for shorts and the sandals for her bare feet. She'd leave through the back door of the old farmhouse, cut across the mielie fields, and, when she came to the crossroads where the tar road from Wintertown central changed into hard red dirt, she'd run.

She'd start slow, walking faster and faster until that moment when she'd fly, her bare feet slap-

slapping as the wind gathered speed around her, blowing away the shame, the disappointment and, yes, the disgust she saw shadowing Ma's eyes until nothing existed except her easy breathing and the silence.

She never knew how long she ran each day. She never knew that people saw her flying along the road, her arms pumping as her long stride ate up the kilometres, her eyes focused on a point only she could see, until she arrived home that Wednesday afternoon to find Mr de Koker, Wintertown Hoërskool's sports master, waiting on the stoep with Ma and Pa.

'Good afternoon, sir,' she said, hovering at the bottom of the stoep stairs, close to where Pa sat, his big square hand, so similar to her own, lazily stroking Hond's ear.

'Middag, meisie,' the teacher replied. 'How far did you run today?'

Surprised at the question, Johanna shrugged. 'I don't remember.' Her anxiety made her voice deeper than usual, and knowing how Ma hated it, she shifted uneasily, her bare toes digging into the tired patch of grass Ma insisted was their front lawn. 'I ran from the crossroads to the top of Platberg, past Wimpy Burgers, down Main Road and then back to the farm along the ox trail.'

'That's nearly twenty kilometres! I saw you at the crossroads at 2 o'clock.' Mr de Kocker checked his watch, the one he'd bought on Amazon, Ma said one Saturday afternoon after Bible class, the chrome-and-black sports watch newsworthy because Sannie from the post office told the bible ladies that the small parcel from America was the first Wintertown online purchase.

Mr de Koker let out a long, slow whistle. 'That's about 5 minutes a kilometre! For a girl!'

Ma stiffened. 'What does that mean?' Johanna could only drop her eyes in shame. 'Jammer, Meneer,' she apologised. 'I didn't push myself today.'

'You didn't push yourself?' Mr de Koker gave a snort of joy. 'I'd like to see you push yourself! But not yet. No, no, not yet. First, we need a sponsor … maybe Mayor Radebe will help. The town council must have funds—'

'What are you talking about?' Ma asked, looking as confused as Johanna felt.

Mr de Koker took a deep breath. 'Koba, your daughter is the most talented long-distance runner I've seen. And she's only seventeen!'

'You're stuck at Wintertown Hoërskool.' Pa, a man of few words, spoke out from the bottom of the stoep stairs where he sat, still stroking Hond's ears, lifting and flopping, lifting and flopping. 'You can't have seen many long-distance runners.'

Mr de Koker, his chubby face flushed with annoyance, said, 'I've worked as an official at national track meets, Johan. I know runners. And Johanna is good. More than good…she can beat the best in the world if she wants to.'

'Is that what you want, *Poppie*?' Pa asked, looking at Johanna.

In her head, Johanna heard crowds cheering, as they did for those runners on the TV when she watched SuperSport on the weekends, while Pa sat next to her doing the crosswords, and Ma drove into Wintertown for her Bible class and the week's gossip.

The imaginary cheers didn't make Johanna think about winning a race or making a fortune. Those cheers meant acceptance: no more laughter at the silly pink dresses she wore, at her too-deep voice or the hair on her legs and under her arms, which grew thickly until Ma took her to Tannie Bessie's Salon.

The salon wasn't really a salon; it was a rondavel Oom Piet had built in the backyard once

Tannie Bessie had completed her beautician's course through correspondence with a beauty-and-make-up school back in the days when Pretoria was still called Pretoria and not Tshwane.

'Johanna!' Ma said. 'Your Pa asked you a question.'

Johanna heard Ma's voice faintly through the cheers, rumbling louder and louder in her head. Her heart beat faster, and her breath got short with excitement. Let them laugh at me when I wear gold, she thought and looked Pa straight in the eye. 'I want to run,' she said. 'I only want to run.'

Things moved quickly after that, even though Ma wasn't happy.

'She'll have to have her own changing room,' Ma said to Mr de Koker. 'She's very shy,' although Johanna knew the real reason was that Ma didn't want anyone to find out that she wasn't just a girl; she had boy parts in her body, too.

'I'll see what I can do,' Mr de Koker promised.

Privately, Ma gave Johanna instructions. 'Don't bend over in front of the other girls,' she said. 'And always wear your broekies, even in the shower.'

Mr de Koker kept his word. As Johanna ran her way into the record books, first as school champion, then provincial champion, and then as national champion, Mr de Koker always found her a private area to change. The other girls on the team didn't like it, but Mr de Koker heard the envy in their whispers, and he knew it was Johanna's talent they didn't like. So he smiled and soothed and still organised Johanna's private changing area, even when she went to the World Championships, running her way into the world's record books in the final heat.

GIRL WONDER.

That's what they called her first.

Good or bad, Johanna had learned early not to care what they called her. All she cared about now was the wind rushing through her hair, the gold medals building up enough glitter to blind all that pink back in her room at the old farmhouse in Wintertown, and running, always running, into the cheers of the crowds on her way to the Olympics, which offered the brightest gold of them all.

FLYING FREAK

That's what they called her next.

Her heavy face and square hands, big and strong like Pa's when he worked the land, her flat chest and her speed … oh, her speed that was cheetah fast, faster than all the female athletes and faster than most of the male athletes too — all that started the whispers again.

Mary Jones, America's hope for gold in the next Olympics, whispered the loudest. 'Just look at her! She's not a woman; she's a man in disguise.'

America's pride jogged around in a circle, her arms flapping like awkward wings as the rest of Johanna's competitors, all of whom she'd beaten at one point or another, howled with laughter. 'Or she's a freak, a flying freak.'

Johanna heard them and recognised the sound. Mr de Koker, now her personal coach, found her on the track, running the laughter away.

She couldn't run away from the letter that had arrived. The AIF logo was easily recognisable with its stylised athlete victorious on a bright red-and-yellow track.

'Dear Ms Venter

Gender Verification Test

The Athletics International Federation has received notification that, for a female athlete, your:

> *(i) physique is too masculine*
> *(ii) muscles are too pronounced*
> *(iii) stride is too long for your height*

You are hereby advised to present yourself on Tuesday, 28ᵗʰ February at 09h00 at the Sports Clinic at Randburg, Johannesburg. A medical representative of the AIF will verify that your gender is female. Once verified, you will be issued an official AIF Gender Verification Pass, which you will be required to present at future athletic championships.

Should you refuse to attend the GVT, or should the results show that you are not female, you will no longer be eligible to compete.'

Johanna took the letter to Mr de Koker, who read it slowly, rubbing the side of his nose until it shone red. He was silent for so long Johanna worried that he was wondering about Ma's insistence on a private dressing room. But, even though Ma had said that everyone knew Mr de Koker lived with his male friend and had never had a girlfriend, not even when he attended Wintertown Hoërskool as a pupil, Johanna could still not bring herself to tell him that she was both boy and girl.

Perhaps, she hoped, like the doctor who helped Ma at her birth, the AIF doctor wouldn't notice that tiny penis that had loomed so large in her life. Perhaps, she thought, although she might be both boy and girl in body, they would only see that inner flame driving her to run as fast and as hard as she could.

'I'm a girl, Meneer,' was all she could say as Mr de Koker stood there holding the AIF letter.

He shook himself out of his trance, slinging a comforting arm around her shoulder. 'I know, Jo,' he said, 'you're a girl wonder!'

Sounding as if he knew more than she wanted him to, he folded the letter neatly and, tucking it into his pocket, said, 'They won't get away with this, Johanna. You'll still run for as long as you can.' His voice was so determined, so fierce, she believed him.

The clinic was cold. With her AIF badge, hard eyes behind rimless spectacles, and plastic-gloved hands, the doctor was even colder than the grey walls and threadbare carpet.

'Leave her with me,' she said to Mr de Koker. 'This could take all morning — there are several gender verification tests. The physical exam, the blood tests, ultrasound.'

'Surely the physical exam isn't necessary,' Mr de Koker protested. 'She's a young girl.'

'The tests will tell us what the gender is,' the doctor said. 'The nurse will be present at all times. You can return later.'

'Meneer!' Johanna cried, her heart pumping, not in the good way when she ran, but in a bad way, scurrying around inside her chest the same as it had done when the Wintertown girls had gathered around her with their taunts and their laughter.

'He must leave,' the doctor said. 'It's the rules.' After pushing him from the room, she pointed to a curtained bed. 'Strip. Use the gown hanging there, and call me when you're ready.'

Pushing her glasses back up her nose, she sat at her desk and began filling out a form. Johanna hovered, Ma's voice, telling her never to strip off completely, loud in her head, competing with her fear of what would happen if she refused to obey the doctor.

'Well, what are you waiting for?' the doctor asked when Johanna didn't move. 'Get moving, I haven't got all day!'

The gown was, of course, pink. There were no buttons, only a loose tie so the doctor could easily access Johanna's shivering body.

The doctor never said another word to Johanna during the next three hours. She prodded, poked, and pricked; the only sound she made was when she opened Johanna's legs.

'Aaah!' the doctor said to the also-silent nurse, who had swabbed Johanna's bare skin, readying it for the needle jabs and spreading gel on Johanna's pelvis so the rubber pad of the ultrasound could slither coldly over her belly, the twisted cord like a mamba waiting to strike. 'Look at this, Sister!'

Johanna closed her eyes tightly, breathing hard to keep from crying as the doctor's gloved finger found the little penis that was Ma's worst nightmare and Johanna's everlasting shame.

'We'll see what the chromosome and hormone tests say, but this is an open and shut case of gender fraud,' the doctor said. She slapped Johanna's knees back together. 'Get dressed. I'll speak to your coach — you're a disgrace to your sport and your country!'

Johanna couldn't hold the tears back. When Mr de Koker found her shivering and sobbing in the pink hospital gown, he rested a comforting hand on her shoulder before calling a nurse to help her change back into her clothes. Then he took her home to Wintertown.

The next day, the doctor's report went viral.

America's Olympic hope was gleefully quoted. 'I knew all along she wasn't normal. She's more man than woman,' Mary Jones said, 'and freaks shouldn't run with us.'

For Johanna, hiding in her pink bedroom, all the gold medals Pa had hung up next to the cut-out clownfish and over Alfie, the African land snail's, tank meant nothing. She could only cry for all the shame she had brought on Ma now that the whole world knew her secret.

'*Poppie*,' Pa said, striding into her room, his usually placid face pinched and angry. 'Stop this nonsense. Crying doesn't solve anything.' He pulled out a pink jersey and Johanna's favourite jeans. 'Get dressed,' he said. 'Meneer de Koker is here — the press wants to interview you.'

Pa wouldn't take no for an answer, and after shepherding her onto the stoep, he refused to leave. 'I'm angry,' Pa said, glaring at the strangers filling the stoep chairs. 'I'm furious. Nature mixes things up, sometimes. You say my child is not a girl? Hah! Go to her room, take pictures with your fancy blerry cameras, and make sure they're in colour! Anyone here in Wintertown will tell you pink is my Johanna's favourite colour.' Pa banged his hand against his heart. 'In here, where it counts, she's a girl.'

Satisfied, Pa sat back, his big hand, hard and calloused from a lifetime of working the land, dropping automatically to stroke Hond's head, silencing the dog's low growl. 'And I'm telling you now, we're laying a charge against those people for their stupidity!'

The hungry journalists bayed with excitement, but Pa had had his say.

Mr de Koker took over, reading the details from a paper he had kept in his pocket. 'On Monday, 12th July, the Human Rights Commission of South Africa laid a complaint of discrimination and human rights abuse against the Athletics International Federation with the United Nations Human Rights Council. The unwarranted and invasive scrutiny of the intimate details of South African athlete Johanna Albertina Venter's body is both sexist and an abuse of her basic human right to privacy.'

The press pack went wild.

The AIF stripped Johanna of her medals, banning her from any international competitions until, they said in their press statement, "further gender verification tests were completed."

The public went wild.

The Mother of the Nation and her entourage drove through the streets of Wintertown, out to the Venter farm, where she hugged Johanna and told her how proud the nation was of her and the gold medals she had won.

'We must stand by this child of ours,' the Mother of the Nation said. 'None of us is free if even one of us is still suffering in the chains of discrimination and abuse.'

The country heeded the call. South Africa's Venter would not be discarded, her life ruined, like India's Soundarajan or Spain's Patiño.

GIRL WONDER fan clubs sprang up on Facebook and Twitter. Johanna was invited to speak at schools, and clubs, and conferences across the country. The young girls, who weren't all girls, and the boys, who weren't all boys, wrote letters to her saying, 'You're our star, Johanna.'

At the next Olympics, America's best hope was nowhere to be seen, banned for using anabolic steroids. Johanna walked into the stadium leading the South African Olympics squad, her muscular arms carrying the flag, its bright rainbow colours weaving through the air as she proudly shouldered its weight.

She knew her fight wasn't over: the AIF had advised Mr de Koker that they were implementing a rule that would force Johanna to submit to medical correction or be banned for life.

That was a different battle, one she would look to in the future. On this night, her Olympic debut night, Johanna just ran. She ran as fast as she had ever run, for now, her running had a reason: she was doing it for them.

She was running for all those ordinary, fragile souls whose bodies had been shamed like hers. In them, she had found herself. And so she ran for them, for those who, like her, had found comfort only in cut-out posters of clownfish. Now they had a different poster they could dream about: an athlete, an international star, her body neither fully boy nor fully girl, but simply the body of Johanna Venter, Girl Wonder.

Who Let the Dog Out

☐   'Ambrose, dinner is ready,' Susan called.

When Ambrose didn't answer, she walked from the kitchen to the living room, her sensible brown shoes clacking noisily against the new vinyl tiles, patterned to look like a natural wooden floor. She found him in front of the new television set Benjamin had proudly brought home two months earlier. Ambrose lay on the floor, long, pointed chin resting in hands too large for his size and age, his shaggy blonde-brown hair hanging over his eyes glued to the images of a collie dog and its adventures.

With the bonus he'd received for being the best bank teller of the year, Ambrose's father had paid cash for the seventeen-inch Crosley colour television set, cradled in a shiny mahogany wood veneer cabinet. Susan preferred the blond wood veneer to match the kitchen floor vinyl tiles.

Still, Benjamin had been so proud, and Ambrose so excited, that she'd immediately moved the large walnut display cabinet that had stood in pride of place in the living room into the kitchen. Susan loved that cabinet, even though the little brass key no longer worked, and one corner of the bevelled green glass top was jagged and chipped. She'd inherited it from her mother, who'd inherited it from her mother, and it was the only piece of real wood furniture they owned.

At least in the kitchen, she could still stroke the hand-carved flowers decorating the corners, touching each petal delicately, like a fragile blossom easily crushed. She'd already got used to the big television dominating the living room, and Ambrose, her last born, her strange child with dreamy brown eyes filled with the sorrows of the world, spent as much of his days as he could immersed in the coloured images flickering across the small screen.

'I'm coming, Mama,' he said, not taking his tearful eyes off the screen where Lassie and Timmy were racing against time to save an injured police dog.

Susan, wiping her hands on her apron, shook her head with no real annoyance. She was pleased Ben had chosen the TV rather than the washing machine. From when he'd first switched on the set and Ambrose had discovered the Lassie series, Susan always knew where she would find her son.

'Look, Mamma,' Ambrose said. 'I can roll over like Lassie!' He rolled over on his back, shaking his skinny arms and legs in the air, his bare feet dirty because she could never get him to keep his shoes on.

Susan laughed at his antics to make him happy, but she worried about his future. Everyone kept telling her Ambrose was a little strange.

'He's just a little…different,' Susan liked to correct them. 'There's no harm in him,' she'd say. 'He's like an overgrown puppy still learning social skills.'

Oh, he didn't like strangers coming into their small yard, and when friends came over for Sunday lunch, piling out of their cars, loaded with children, potato salads and cold beers, Ambrose would scamper out on all fours to greet them.

'Woof! Woof!' he'd say, rising on his knees, his hands pawing the air as he made barking noises.

Some friends, embarrassed and unsure how to respond, ignored him. Others, much to Ambrose's delight, would play along.

'Good boy, Ambrose,' they'd say, laughing at his silliness. 'Good boy!' as if Ambrose really was a dog.

In a frenzy of excitement at the attention, Ambrose would throw himself on the grass, make whining noises, wiggling his bottom until he was given a belly rub.

When he was a toddler, his dog imitation was endearing. The older he grew, even Susan had to admit that Ambrose was more than a little strange.

'Susan,' Mrs Linton, the headmistress, said, 'Ambrose is a sweet child.'

'He is a special little boy, isn't he?' Susan smiled, her right hand creeping up to twist the small pearl necklace Ben had given her on their wedding day. She only wore it for special occasions, but tonight, at the first parent-teacher evening since Ambrose started school, some vague unease had made her wear it. For good luck, some part of her thought.

'He is that, indeed.' Mrs Linton hesitated, an awkward silence stretching between them as she searched for the right way to say what she had to say. 'Ambrose is such a bright little boy — gifted in many ways. And he's very obedient, too. When I tell him to stop licking the children, he stops immediately. But…there's something a little odd that's upsetting the others.'

'I know he's a little different,' Susan said. 'Only…he's such a sweet, friendly child, so willing to help, especially with the smaller children. Have you noticed how he always seems to gravitate to the children who need cheering up?' Susan asked the teacher eagerly. 'Somehow, when he rubs against them, he comforts them, and they always smile.'

Mrs Linton clutched the clipboard tighter before plunging in, the words tumbling from her mouth in a nervous rush. 'Ambrose really needs help! He's disruptive! He refuses to sit at a desk – he'll only sit on the floor – on his hands and knees!' As hard as she tried to stay as professional as a headmistress should, her voice rose an indignant notch. 'The worst of it is…I've had complaints…I don't know how to say this…his bathroom habits are causing the biggest problems!'

Susan closed her eyes briefly as her heart cracked a little. She'd known she was too easy on Ambrose, but she'd thought — prayed every night — he'd outgrow the dog phase, especially once he started school.

'Wha-what's Ambrose doing now?' she asked, not daring to look at Ben, who, for months, had been telling her she should be stricter with the boy. But she hadn't been able to steal Ambrose's joy from him: his delight in playing Lassie; his full-hearted immersion in the fictional dog's adventures made him happy, and he wasn't a nasty, horrible child. He was like sunshine, spreading light and laughter when life seemed too hard to bear.

'He thinks he's a dog!' Mrs Linton said.

'Oh, is that all?' Susan gave a huff of relief. 'It's a phase he'll grow out of.'

'He's getting worse, not better,' Mrs Linton said firmly as if she was talking to one of the first graders rather than a parent. 'He begs for food. The other children think it's a joke, but some are starting to get very uncomfortable. He can't go on like this. He must behave normally, like all the others!'

And so began the rehabilitation of Ambrose from a dog spirit into what was considered ordinary by the powers that be. Susan and Ben started punishing Ambrose every time he acted like a dog.

Susan knew she was doing what she had to do to make Ambrose fit into the society in which he lived, but tucked away in her mother's heart, a part of her wept every time she punished Ambrose for being himself. She hardened that heart and, for his sake, ignored how, with every punishment, the light of his gentle soul dimmed a little more. Slowly, over time, the sunny cheerfulness that was so much part of Ambrose disappeared. Like a dog chained and prevented from running free, Ambrose grew into a snarling and snapping teenager isolated from and rejecting anyone approaching him.

At his junior school graduation, Mrs Linton congratulated Susan and Ben. 'You've done an excellent job on Ambrose,' she gushed. 'He's just like all the other kids in his class.'

'He's surly all the time,' Susan replied, trying not to remember how happy Ambrose had once been. 'If we discipline him, he growls at us and runs into his room. He never did that when we let him be a dog.'

'That conduct is nothing to worry about,' said Mrs Linton, beaming. 'He's behaving like every teenager who's ever come through my classroom!'

'Ambrose was never like all the others,' Susan mumbled.

A slight frown creased the heavy makeup on Mrs Linton's face. 'Now, now, Susan,' she said. 'He fits in perfectly with the other students. He won't have any problems as a senior. You've done a great job fixing Ambrose; he'll thank you later. I can't tell you how much easier it is for us at the school now that he behaves like everyone else!'

Eventually, as Ambrose grew into a college teenager, feeding into the University first-year students, disappearing into the masses of students, all filled with plans and hopes and dreams of changing the world, of being a famous politician, a famous scientist or a famous musician, Susan managed to silence that voice in her heart. She watched contentedly as Ambrose plodded along, never failing but never shining brightly like the student stars, those young men and women who always seemed to know precisely who they were, where they were going, and what they were entitled to.

Ben had never been prouder of his son than when he found Ambrose a job as a junior clerk in the same branch of The Home Bank he'd worked in for twenty years. Ben had never understood the joy of Ambrose, the dog child, in the same way that Susan had. Ambrose had embarrassed him as a child, but once they'd fixed him, Ben enjoyed sitting around the Sunday barbecue with his buddies, lovingly complaining about his teenage son.

'Modern kids,' the huddle of Dads would declare, as fathers have said for generations. 'Not half as tough as they were in our day.'

'They need time in the army to get them straight.'

'More discipline, sure, that's what they need.'

Ben would nod, the can in his left hand sweating ice-cold droplets as he flipped the meat on the fire with the tongs he held in his right hand, and they'd all raise their beers, content they'd done their best for their sons.

As he watched a morose and silent Ambrose – grown taller than him now — awkwardly mingle, Ben's gut would give a spasm he'd blame on too many crisps and peanuts.

In those moments, standing around the flickering fire with the other fathers, Ben felt Susan was correct. They'd lost something precious. As the men clung to their comfortable lives and the small victories over one another, boasting how their children were progressing, climbing higher and higher through the system, making more money, buying more cars and planning better marriages, Ben silenced his suffering heart.

'Except Ambrose,' he'd say with a guffaw. 'Ambrose only knows how to plod.'

Ambrose plodded into marriage with Brenda.

Susan never really liked Brenda because she bullied Ambrose. Her daughter-in-law was one of those small women, bird-like in her appearance but tough as steel. Any conversation with her was littered with 'Ambrose said this…' and 'Ambrose said that…', but Susan knew Brenda made the decisions.

Ambrose just plodded along, even his shaggy blonde-brown hair limp and lifeless where once it had shone with good health.

'Are you happy?' Susan would ask.

'I'm content with my life, Mama,' he'd say quietly. 'Brenda is a good wife. She makes my favourite meals, and we do things together.'

'But are you happy?' Some vague memory, some vague anxiety she couldn't quite remember, prodded Susan's heart and kept a niggle of worry alive every time she watched Ambrose jump to do Brenda's bidding.

When she looked at her grown son, Susan saw that same placid, easy-going Ambrose she remembered from his childhood. But she'd never again seen the same happiness in his eyes as when he'd watched Lassie running across the screen of the old television set Ben had long since replaced with a smarter, newer, bigger one.

Ben told her she was worrying for nothing, that every mother of every son in the world thought the woman her son married wasn't good enough. Then, three days before Ambrose's forty-second birthday, Brenda ran off with the used car salesman.

When Susan answered Ben's new banana phone — she hated the strange shape, not entirely trusting that it would work without a telephone wire, but Ben said now he was a bank manager, a modern mobile phone was a necessity —she knew something had happened the moment Ambrose spoke.

'Mama,' Ambrose said.

'What is it, Ambrose?' Susan asked, her mind racing with a million worries. 'What's happened?'

'Brenda has gone, Mama. She's left me.' His voice wobbled. Then he said, so quietly she could hardly hear him, 'Help me.'

No mother who loved her child could bear the sound of her child's sadness.

'I'm coming,' she yelled into the cold, plastic handset she held. What she wanted to hold onto was her son, lost and alone at the other end. Susan never heard the clatter of the mobile phone shattering on the floor. Scrabbling for her car keys — why were they always at the bottom of her purse, buried under tissues and gum and lipstick when she needed them in a hurry? — 'I'm going to Ambrose's house,' Susan shouted to Ben, watching Saturday Morning Live in the striped pyjamas Brenda and Ambrose had given him for his birthday. If he responded, she never knew, for she was already in the car on her way to Ambrose.

Susan found him sitting at the pine wooden table in the kitchen, the green plastic tablecloth with embossed pink proteas covered in crumbs and dried gravy, the condiments in the middle of the table looking as lost and forlorn, as abandoned and unwanted as her poor son.

'What happened, Ambrose?' Susan flung her purse onto the table and drew his head against her bosom, stroking his short, spikey hair, remembering how soft and shaggy it once was.

'Mama,' he said, his hand with its short, blunt fingers and long nails clutching her waist. 'Mama, Brenda said I couldn't make her happy. She said I was always too sad, and Joe—' he gulped air, gathering the courage to go on.

'Joe? Joe Papagiano, the used car salesman?' Susan asked. 'She left you for that lying shark?'

'He makes her laugh. Why can't I make people laugh anymore, Mama? At the bank, I do everything I'm told, but I haven't got any friends. I did anything Brenda asked me to, whatever she wanted and —' he pushed his head deeper into the safety of her embrace, 'I couldn't make her happy! Is it me, Mama? Is it because I don't know how to be happy anymore?'

Tears flooded Susan's eyes, springing from the depth of Ambrose's sorrow and her memory of when Ambrose was a light shining in everyone's life.

When he pawed at their shoes or sat up and begged at the table, most people — not all, but most people — laughed and, after bending down to pat him, had turned away, a little lighter in spirit because of the sheer joy emanating from her strange dog-child.

The bliss shining from Ambrose as he'd rushed around the garden, making barking noises and chasing imaginary butterflies before rolling in the grass, panting happily, had brought such pleasure to their friends and to Ambrose himself. If she wanted to be honest with herself, Susan had also preferred Ambrose, the dog child, to the sad shadow of a man who clung so desperately to her, broken and lost and not knowing what happiness life could hold.

'I know what the answer is,' she said. 'You need to let the dog out!'

Deep in Ambrose's soft brown eyes, a light started shining again.

'Yes! Oh yes, Mama! That's what I must do! I've forgotten who I am.' Ambrose jumped up from the chair, his shoulders no longer stooped, standing taller than he had for years. 'Now I remember!' he shouted, and Susan saw the first glimmers of the joyous child he'd once been.

'This time,' she said, the guilt she'd carried all those years before she'd forgotten what they had done when Ambrose started school at last easing, 'we'll do it properly!'

Before long, she was helping him prepare a dog suit.

'What breed do you want to be?' Susan asked Ambrose, knowing the answer.

'A Lassie, Mama!'

'Right then, a rough collie it is!'

Together, they found a way to create a wire skeleton shaped like a dog. Armed with his measurements, Susan went to every sewing shop she could, examining all the faux fur samples they had until she found a material that wasn't only the perfect tan-and-white colour but was soft enough and long enough to blow in the wind as naturally as Lassie's shiny coat flowed as she ran.

'What about his hands and knees?' Ben asked. At first, he'd refused anything to do with the idea, but Ambrose's excitement spilled over, and soon he offered advice. 'And how is the costume going to stay on?'

While Ben built a harness to keep the furry costume firmly attached to Ambrose's body, Susan spent days finding clear plastic sandals that would work as paws. She painted on claws and used soft foam rubber as claw pads. They built a papier-mâché mask with a long collie face, tufty ears covered in faux fur and holes where Ambrose's gentle brown eyes could shine through.

Ambrose needed only a few practice runs before he mastered walking and rolling and pawing the air in the costume.

'He's a natural,' Susan said, clapping her hands. From the smile on Ben's face, she saw that he was just as proud of Ambrose as she was.

Then, it was time for Ambrose to go on his first dog walk. Carefully, he stepped into the costume before dropping to his hands and knees so that she could put a shiny red collar on him, one with a reflective band for safety and a small disc with his name and Ben's mobile number on it, clicking the leash into place.

'Come, boy,' she said. 'There's nothing to be afraid of. Mama's with you.'

Ambrose needed some coaxing before he walked outside the gate. He scampered to hide behind the small blue Fiat parked in the street, hunching down behind the tyre. Nothing Susan said could get him to move until a young child walked by.

'Look, Mummy,' she said, tugging her mother's hand until she was close enough to pat Ambrose. 'A doggie!' She looked up at Susan, jerking the leash between her hands as she noticed the child's mother give Ambrose a strange look. 'Is he your doggie?' the child asked, blue eyes shining with happiness.

'He's my precious boy,' Susan said. 'He's very friendly but a bit shy. Why don't you pat him?'

'He's a big doggie! Will he bite?'

'Woof!' Ambrose said, shaking his papier-mâché head.

'Ambrose,' Susan said, 'Shake paws with the little girl.'

'My son,' Susan said to reassure the girl's mother, 'is just a little…different. All he wants to do is make people happy.'

Joy filled the next ten minutes as Ambrose shook paws, rolled over for belly rubs, and rested his large, shaggy head on the child's shoes. He even drew a tentative smile from the girl's mother as he sat up and begged in front of her.

'Good boy,' she said, cautiously patting his furry head.

'Woof! Woof!' said Ambrose, and everyone laughed.

After that first dog walk, Susan would meet Ambrose every Saturday and Sunday.

'When I'm in the stuffy old bank, I think about wearing my real clothes all the time, Mama,' he said as she helped him climb into his dog costume.

'And, Mama, do you want to know what happens when I think about being in my real clothes?'

'Tell me, Ambrose,' Susan said.

'Everyone smiles at me now, Mama!' Ambrose laughed. 'Everyone says just looking at me makes them happy.'

Deep in her mother's heart, Susan knew that what made everyone smile at Ambrose during those long, unbearably stifling weekdays when he had to do everything by the rules was because his heart and soul were once again alight with joy.

Some people called embracing Ambrose's true doggie self a form of lunacy. Susan, however, thought the craziness of his dogdom was irrelevant. All that mattered was how happy Ambrose was. And how, in a world filled with the chaos and destruction they saw every night on their big television screen, his happiness was a beacon for all those who, having lost a sense of their true selves, found in meeting Ambrose, the dog child, the courage to follow the light out of their own darkness.

The Leopard and the Lizard

In the manner peculiar to the African bushveld, the blood-orange sun sinks quickly, dropping below the solitary line of akasia trees standing sentinel on the horizon.

Still, the two men don't move—not even when the cry of the first jackal sends blistering fingers down their spines, curling fear and anticipation into their bellies. They've waited many years for this night— years that have passed too quickly and too slowly.

A small herd of impala grazing at the edge of the camp looks at them with careful eyes as the setting sun brushes the last warmth from the day. The black-haired man stands up abruptly, an unwilling smile finding its way to his face as the impala skitter gracefully away, seeking the safety of the dense bush beyond their view.

'Are you ready?' he asks. Almost without waiting for his grey-haired brother's nod, he picks up the drum, easily letting the heavy throb dance through his fingers in concert with the flickering fire at his feet.

'Stop now,' his twin says. 'You'll scare them away. We must wait.'

He nods and, regretfully, puts the instrument aside. They sit in silence, the fire dimming, their thoughts locked inside as they wait for the Great Watcher and her companion to arrive.

Time stretches and pulls, the very air around them twanging with the hum of hidden dreams and broken promises. Black John says bitterly, 'They lied.'

'They'll be here,' Grey John reassures softly, as was his wont. 'Don't give up hope.'

'I have no hope,' Black John sneers. 'Hope is for fools.'

'You don't mean that.'

'I do.' Black John shifts sullenly, hunching a shoulder against the rustling air. His brother is a fool and, as he'd promised years—or was it aeons?—ago, tonight will show Grey John what a fool he is. 'We should have killed them then.' He pauses, the fire reflecting the calculating gleam in his eyes. 'Perhaps we still will. Leopard pelts are in demand these days.' His fingers scrabble lazily in the dirt, finding and then sensuously smoothing a small round pebble. 'The lizard is too small. It's useless.'

'Salamander.'

'What?'

'It's a salamander,' Grey John says patiently.

'Whatever.' With a sharp snap of his wrist, Black John spins the pebble into the glowing embers, enjoying the feel of his muscles rippling and the satisfying hiss as another log collapses under the assault. 'There's no money to be made from it. It's too small to make a difference.'

'A single thread can make a difference to the cloth it holds together.'

'You're wrong.'

'We'll see.' Grey John finally stands up. There is no difference between the two men save for the colour of their hair and a gentleness about the eyes Black John lost long ago.

Arching his arms back over his head to ease the ache of waiting, Grey John turns in a slow circle.

'We are born one,' he says, 'and we will die as one. Why have you fought it for so long?'

'The only thing I've fought is my way to the top.'

'She gave you the victory she promised.'

'The Leopard gave me nothing. Whatever I got, I worked for.' Black John pushes himself to his feet, his chin aggressively angled towards his brother. 'It's *my* success—not hers.'

'It's yours, alright,' Grey John murmurs wryly. 'But is it success?'

'What do you know about success? No one listens to your songs. No one even sings them. Yet, you continue to *hope* that they will. That's not success! Do you want to know what success really is?' his brother demands. 'I can do *that*,' he snaps his fingers, the click loud in the silence of the starlit night, 'and a hundred people will jump to obey me.' He strides to the dying fire, kicking it to life again. 'Don't tell me it's not success when you have nothing compared with me.'

'I have hope.'

'Fools have hope. It's all they've got.'

'It is enough.'

'For you, maybe.'

'For you too, if you'd let it.'

Black John has had enough. 'This is ridiculous. We've waited forever; there's nothing for us here. It was just a stupid kid's dream. A fantasy.'

'Why are you so afraid?' Grey John knows why. Watching a nightjar rise from the undergrowth with puffed feathers and an agitated trill, he wonders if his brother knows.

'I'm not afraid. I'm bored.'

'Not for much longer.' He dusts a hand across Black John's shoulder, nodding towards the path the little bird has flown from. 'They come,' he whispers, and, despite his knowing, he feels the lick of anxiety burst into a flame of fear. Will tonight show Black John the way? Or is he lost until another age?

Then, all thought is washed from his mind as the cicadas fall still, the air hovering tautly as they wait.

Into this dense silence comes the Great Watcher, paws puffing up plumes of dust in an even greater silence. The rosettes on her pelt are dark and perfect, a hundred and more eyes staring in every direction, seeking, watching, carefully cataloguing every tiny corruption in the hearts of men who promise friendship and deliver only lies.

Her cold, liquid eyes draw the twins closer together as she pads with effortless grace towards them. Dark yellow shards look contemptuously at Black John until he stutters accusingly, 'You're l-late.'

Settling herself in the centre of their makeshift *boma* with all the feline grace inherent in her species, she slowly, with delicate roughness, rasps her tongue over her pelt. She sees how Black John's eyes greedily scan the perfection of her skin.

'Where's the lizard?' he asks. The leopard ignores him and, with a lazy suddenness, unsheathes her claws, apparently intent only on capturing the last hidden burr knotting her fur and marring her beauty.

It annoys Black John, as she'd known it would.

'We've waited forever for you to come.' He slants his fists into the pockets of his trousers and, in his foolish arrogance, takes a step closer. 'When is the lizard arriving so we can begin?'

'Salamander,' the other one says quietly, drawing her wary eyes towards him. 'How many times must I tell you that?'

The grey-haired, silent one makes her nervous. He makes her question her dark power—she's not used to that. As he swivels his head to look at her directly, she knows tonight will test her to the full.

'Greetings, O Great One,' the quiet man says. 'I've looked forward to this night.'

A shiver slides through her body. She stops playing, determined to show him the full force of her strength. Then he will worship her. Then he will fear her and desire her, as his brother —a man too eager to taste all this life has to offer—does.

Lifting her lips back from the teeth that could easily tear his throat out, she lets the growl echo out of her jaws, proclaiming her greatness to those who can hear and those who choose not to hear, the danger hidden in its seductive promise. The ground beneath her paws trembles, and she is pleased.

Black John pales, stepping closer to the fire and wiping his palms down the sides of his trousers.

As if that will save him, she smiles secretly *when the time comes for him to pay me.*

'That was...impressive,' Grey John says.

She grumbles a snarl at him, not trusting the mildness in his voice. Over the years, she's placed temptation after temptation before him, and always he has that same look of resolute meekness about him. The one that makes her wonder where he gets the strength to withstand her and all that she offers him. It's the lizard's fault.

As if her thoughts conjure the creature, it scampers into the clearing. So ugly compared with her. So little, she can crush it with one paw.

'You're late, Lizard.' She hates that she sounds as petulant as Black John.

'Salamander,' Grey John corrects and starts towards her.

She half rises, the multitude of black eyes rippling into watchfulness over her muscled haunches, bunched now in readiness to strike any threat Grey John offers. He passes her by, and she sinks uneasily back into the dirt.

Gently picking up the cold, small body of the reptile, he says, 'I'm glad you came.'

The salamander scrambles up his arm to lie panting on his shoulder, looking down at her with eyes that have endured much. Its tail cupping Grey

John's neck like a lover's sweet hand, unwilling to let go, the creature says, 'It's time. Who shall begin?'

The leopard stands up arrogantly. 'It is my right.'

'Says who?' Black John objects.

'Be quiet,' she says, staring at him with casual cruelty in her eyes. 'Tonight, you finally belong to me.' His gaze falls first. 'Sit,' she orders, and Black John drops like a ripe marula berry to the ground.

'Many cycles of the moon have passed,' she begins, once Black John stops wriggling his legs to find a comfortable position, 'since we four last met. You were both black-haired boys, identical in nature and in form. Each of you, so full of pride, felt the fire of longing within.' Her whiskers twitch; anyone who doesn't know her could think she's smiling fondly.

'It amused me,' she continues, 'to see you so sure of your purpose. So certain of what you would do and of what you would not do in your noble pursuits. You were both so young then.'

Her words whisper the memory, drawing the others in with her until, once again, they stand poised on the edge of a doorway into time ...

'Psst! John, do you see that?'

'What? Where?'

'Over there, above the rock in the sun the lizard is lying on.'

'Do you see it?' His fingers fumble slightly in his eagerness, for he's never shot a leopard before. He'll earn a fortune if he can kill it cleanly. He recognises the moment the other boy sees it because he freezes, reverence replacing the sweaty fatigue on his face.

'That...that's the most beautiful animal I've ever seen,' his twin choked, fear and longing vying for supremacy in his voice. 'Don't kill it!'

'Are you mad?' he whispers back. 'Of course, I'm going to kill it! I want its skin—it'll pay the cost of the bike I've been saving for.' As he speaks, he lifts his weapon to his shoulder, fear and nerves forgotten as greed hooks into his heart.

He also forgets that, here, in the busy stillness of the bushveld, the cocking of his weapon is an alien sound. Before he has time to sight the barrel, a mighty roar, like nothing he's ever heard before, rents the air. In a frenzied instant, he could never afterwards recall, the leopard stands over him, her fetid breath clogging his nostrils, her great paws keeping him sprawling helplessly in the dirt.

'Did you think to destroy me?' the leopard mocks. '*You*, of all puny creatures?' The heat of her scorches his skin until slowly, slowly, a chill seeps through his frigid body, quenching the torment in his soul.

Then his brother says, '*I* will kill you if you don't let him go.' The sound of metal scraping on metal makes the leopard swivel her head towards him, where he stands to their left. She looks at him carefully, measuring the coolness in his eyes and the steadiness of his hand, and she knows he'll shoot her before she can reach him.

'Put the gun down,' she purrs, 'and I'll give you anything you want.'

He looks at her in silence, his finger tightening on the trigger.

'Anything,' she whispers and sees a flicker of temptation bite as the barrel of his gun dips minutely.

'How?' the boy asks. 'You're just an animal.'

'Are men not animals, too? I know your secrets, and I have the power you seek.'

'Don't trust her,' a thin whistle from somewhere over to their right warns. 'She'll still get you in the end.'

As the reptile speaks for the first time, a flash of anger tarnishes the dull yellow of the leopard's eyes.

'What does such an ugly little creature know?' she asks, not wanting to lose her hold on him. 'You will live in opulence and power; you can have it all. Money. Wealth. Control. All that they can buy. Just put the gun down.'

The boy looks at the leopard, her ivory teeth scoring scarlet pinpricks across the skin at his brother's throat. He sees the strength in her shoulders, the beauty of her pelt and the power in her paws. He knows he doesn't want to kill her.

Then he looks at the reptile with its cold, shiny skin, its scrawny legs and even scrawnier tail, and he wonders what use such a tiny creature could have in this world.

'What about my brother?'

'He gets nothing. You get it all.' She sees the hunger rise in him and dips her head so he won't see the triumph in her eyes. 'Do you want it?'

'Don't listen to her!' the foolish boy under her paws cries. She stops his protest with a quasi-gentle bite, turning the pinpricks into rivulets of red, pooling stickily in the brown dust beneath his neck.

He groans and lies still. His twin shifts his feet restlessly, the gun in his arms getting heavier. He doesn't know what to do.

'Lizard, will the leopard kill me if I put the gun down?' he asks.

'I'm not a lizard. I'm a salamander.'

'Whatever.' He shrugs, his soul already dreaming of the riches the leopard promises.

'Refuse the Leopard. I will give you something better.'

'What can be better than being successful and rich and having everything I want for all of my life?'

'You decide.' The salamander slithers awkwardly down the rock and stands next to the leopard. 'Look at me,' he says modestly. 'I am small and weak compared with the leopard and all she can offer. But I can give you what she can't.'

'What is that?'

'Hope,' the salamander says. 'I can give you hope.'

'Hope?' The black-haired boy, still as entranced with the leopard's beauty as when his brother pointed her out, is disgusted. 'What use is that?'

'In dark days to come, hope can be your torch.'

'Listen to the salamander!' the trapped boy begs.

He has seen into the leopard's dark heart. When she so casually—so leisurely—tears the skin at his throat, he knows with absolute certainty that if his brother chooses unwisely, her provocative promise will doom them both. In that instant, every hair on his head turns cold stone grey, the colour of the salamander waiting so patiently for an answer.

The leopard sees the boy waver, the gun barrel beginning to lift again. 'Let your brother take the lizard's gift,' she offers generously. 'You can have my gift if you promise to return here when the star of love kisses the moon again. Then we will decide who has best served their purpose.'

'What happens to the one who can find no purpose?' the salamander chimes in.

'I'll eat him, of course.' Her head tilts with amusement, and the leopard stands back, freeing the boy she'd captured. She lies down with elegant ease, majestically folding one foreleg over the other, watching him cough and clutch his throat, still bearing the marks of her teeth. 'Then, he will be mine for all eternity and beyond.' Looking at the boy with the gun, she says. 'Make the promise.'

'I promise,' Black John agrees, knowing he is a sure winner with the leopard's gifts to use as his own.

'I promise,' Grey John cries, hoping he'll have enough time to convince Black John that all is not as it seems. He stands up. Moving to his brother's side, Grey John says, 'We'll be here,' and tugs his brother's arm, pulling him back into their civilised lives, leaving the leopard and the lizard—no! Salamander, he reminds himself—where they belong, deep in the primal bushveld...

'... and so you left us here,' the leopard ends her recollection, 'to start your life's journey. To find your purpose, using only what we each had given you.' She pauses, sensing Black John's rising excitement. 'Do you remember your promise and what it meant?'

'Yes,' Black John says confidently. 'Whoever lost tonight would become yours for eternity.'

'Are you afraid of losing?'

Black John's laughter howls through the night, stopping even the hyenas as they gnaw their way through yesterday's bones. 'How can you even doubt that I've won? Grey John is finished. You can have him,' he says callously. 'I'm tired of his endless whines. *I'm not giving up yet,*' he chants in a parody of his twin's voice. '*There's still hope.*' He snorts rudely. 'Hope? When even a blind man can see he's just a loser!'

Grey John merely smiles, stroking a tender hand over the salamander's body. 'There will be no loser tonight, brother,' he says and, with a sigh, lowers the little creature onto a rock. 'Goodbye, old friend. Thank you.' He's sure the salamander winks at him before scurrying away into a crevice in the rock.

For a moment, he stands still, gathering his strength inwards. Then he squares his shoulders, swinging to face the leopard, which has moved closer to Black John. 'Take me,' he says. 'Give him another chance.'

'No,' the leopard snarls. 'You'll be the death of me yet.'

'Would that be so bad?' Grey John asks mildly.

'Yes. It must be him. He's been mine for an age.' She looks at Black John with such hunger, such greed he trembles in shock.

'What's going on?' The thready sound emerging from his throat isn't like a cry of victory. 'Why does she want *me* when I've won?'

'Oh, you fool!' The leopard's laughter draws the circling hyenas closer and closer. 'Do you not know yet?'

'Know what?' Black John's breath hitches in his throat.

'I've had you all along,' the Great Watcher says, her eyes glittering with ferocious triumph.

Deep in their voracious depths, Black John finally sees the bitter truth. His life means nothing, nothing at all. It has always been without purpose, without meaning. He's betrayed the better part of himself, not for gold, but for dross.

He turns empty eyes towards his brother. '*You* always had hope.' He swallows dryly, his prominent larynx bobbing up and down like a half-eaten apple discarded by children tired of their party games. 'But I had none.'

Grey John's heart clenches painfully at the sight of his brother's tears. He's seen it coming for years. The disillusionment. The loss of all that he thought he was.

And yet...

'There is always hope,' he murmurs softly.

'Is there?' Black John asks him. 'Even for me?'

His brother doesn't know it, but Hope is already alive in his eyes. 'Especially for you.'

'What about her?' Black John squints at the leopard, pacing endlessly around the fire, the swish of her tail almost choking the steadily burning embers into darkness.

'Leave her to me.'

The leopard sees him coming, and she strikes with all the wrath of one who knows her time is over. Once again, she has Grey John by the throat.

This time, he's expecting it. Digging his hands into her neck, he keeps her scent at bay. In a lascivious parody of fleshly union, they twist and turn, edging ever closer to the flames, which leap and roar into new life even as they wait to consume.

Knowing it is the only way, Grey John boldly steps into the fire, the leopard still clasped to his breast. He holds her there until defeat and pique fill her eyes. With a sinuous twist, she drags herself from his hold, yowling as she runs into the bushes, ash and burning embers staining her once beautiful coat.

'You should have killed her!' Black John accuses as his brother stands up, unharmed by the devouring flames. 'With the leopard still alive, how can we be safe from her false promises?'

'I will keep you safe,' says Grey John, his shape beginning to shift as he speaks.

Before Black John's appalled gaze, he changes into a salamander.

'Grey John!' he cries. 'Don't leave me!'

'I will never leave you, my brother,' the salamander comforts. 'Fear not, I will sustain you, for I am always in you.' Then he darts into the night, leaving Black John alone by the dying fire.

For a long while, the man stands dazed and inexplicably frightened until the night's chill penetrates his trance.

He is one again, and the time has come for him to leave this place where he battled for his soul. It is time for him to begin to record simple songs long forgotten—songs that bring joy and hope to a despairing world, songs that will fill his life with purpose.

As he bends to douse the last of the fire's embers with the dregs of his coffee, his reflection in the shiny steel mug captures his eyes. No longer as black as the night, every hair on his head is now an irrevocable cold stone grey.

Call Him Kate

When I was a teenager, I would lie in the
deceiving darkness of the night, dreaming of waking
up with my sister's body. I'd dress in her clothes and
walk down the stairs to the kitchen where Mum stood
in her flowered apron scrambling eggs, and Dad sat
reading the morning newspaper. I'd see myself slide
into the empty chair next to my sister, and they would
say, 'Good morning, Kate, we're so glad Rupert has
left you. Will you have toast with your egg?'

I first met Kate in 1973, when I was five years
old.

'Rupert,' Mum said, shrugging into her
lavender-and-black jacket with practised grace. 'Put
Alice's doll down and tidy up. Quickly now,' she
shooed me toward the bathroom, 'wash your hands
and comb your hair. We're going to Cavendish.'

I knew what that meant. Every Christmas, my
sister Alice and I would each get a new outfit for the
annual family photograph to be included in the
Christmas cards my mother would diligently send out
each year, carefully counting how many and from
whom she received cards in return. Two years without
a return Christmas card, and Mum would strike a
name off the list.

Alice, being younger and a girl, chose first: a
pink dress with a frilly collar and tiny pearl buttons so
pretty Kate awoke for the first time when Mum
handed it to me to carry.

'Mine,' Kate whispered as I stroked a hand
along the softness. 'That's mine.'

When we arrived in the boy's department, with
its dull brown, black or grey shorts and navy-and-
white shirts, I was obdurate.

'But, Rupert,' Mum said, holding the smart grey flannel shorts against a plain white shirt, 'you'll look just like Dad when he leaves for the office.'

'I don't want that ugly thing,' I said. 'I want this one,' and I held out Alice's pink dress.

'Rupert,' Mum said, 'that's a *girl's dress*! You can't wear it.'

'You're Father's little man,' the hovering shop assistant added, patting my cheek affectionately even though her lips were thinned and her eyes hard with something that made me feel bad and wrong and dirty. 'You must buy from the boy's department.'

Before I could stop her, Kate burst into loud, noisy sobs. 'I want a pink dress like Alice's!' I cried until the shop assistant lost patience.

'May I, Madam?' she said to Mum. 'At this age, some boys get confused about clothing, so I know how to deal with the problem.' At Mum's nod, she gripped my arm tightly and dragged me to a rail of boy's shirts. 'Choose one of these. Here,' she dropped my arm and rustled through the rack, 'look at this one. You'll look very handsome in red!'

'I want the pink one,' I sobbed.

'Now see here, young man,' she said, 'boys don't wear girl's dresses. And boys don't cry like naughty babies.' Kate, sensing the pink dress disappearing from our grasp, wailed louder. 'Stop this right now!' the assistant said. 'You're embarrassing your mother and sister!'

'I don't want to wear these,' I gasped, speaking the words Kate whispered in my head. 'They're all so ugly.'

'No, they're not!' she snapped, startling my sobs into a hiccup. Taking advantage of my fright, she pulled Alice's pink dress out of my grasp and handed it to Mum. 'This one will make you look handsome,' and she guided my hand to the red shirt with a little navy anchor stitched on the pocket and a white collar.

'I – I –'

'I won't sell you a pink dress,' she said. 'I'll sell you this—' she forced the red shirt into my hand. 'And this—' she added a pair of grey flannel shorts. 'They're proper clothes for boys! You'll make your mother proud by wearing them.'

I wore that red shirt and the grey shorts for the 1973 Christmas photo. I wore hundreds like them for decades, making my mother proud even as Kate sat locked in my misery.

Over the years, I'd soothe Kate with the occasional secret cross-dressing. But as puberty approached and my body became more masculine, the demands on Kate became agonising: it took more and more effort to make my parents proud, to have them love me.

Kate's only relief was when I lay, shrouded in the comforting darkness of my bedroom, imagining I was dancing across a ballroom floor in a billowing candyfloss creation of silk and feathers. The double life of Kate and Rupert was exhausting, for the only hopes and dreams I could allow myself were the ones other people needed me to have.

Like my father, and my father's father — and my son when he was old enough — I went to school at the elite Bishops. I made everyone proud: cricket captain, rugby captain, debating champion, academic colours and Head Boy. Then I became an *ikey*, studying medicine at UCT before the obligatory national service in the SADF.

During the Border War, the blood, the loss, and the sheer waste of lives on both sides almost made Kate break free.

The army counsellors I spoke to were like the sales assistant when I first met Kate. 'You're a doctor, man! People like you don't do that,' they said. '*Jy's*

opgevok, man — your head's fucked up because of
the war. Just get married; it'll all go away.'

Then, one weekend pass when I went home, I
met Sue and decided my only chance at happiness
was to lock Kate away.

Alice, my sister of the pink dress Kate had so
lusted after, was studying law at UCT by then. A
plain, earnest academic, Alice instantly bonded with a
pretty first-year English student. With her heavy red
hair and blue eyes, her vivaciousness outshining her
slight pug nose and overlarge front teeth, Sue was an
extrovert to my introvert. Alice asked me to
accompany her friend to the student dance as having
only recently moved to Cape Town from upcountry,
Sue still needed a date.

I knew at once that Sue was my soul mate. She
was Kate's soul mate, too, but Sue was conservative
and strictly straight. What chance did Kate have of
winning Sue? What chance did I have of winning her
if I told her about Kate? Only I, Rupert, could win
her, and so I banished Kate forever. Or so I thought.

After I'd *uitklaar'd*, we spent the six months
of our honeymoon travelling around Europe in an old
VW bus. Our son, Andrew, was born when I'd
finished specialising as an orthopaedic surgeon. Our
daughter, Briana, was born two years later, and we
moved into a double-story house in upmarket
Rondebosch. The years swept by as swiftly as the
clouds dispersed over Lion's Head on a blustery
winter's day, and soon, there were weddings to
celebrate and the birth of our first granddaughter.

Kate, living all those years in darkness,
became a heavy secret. I carried her, buried deep
within, carefully hidden, always keeping a part of me
aloof. That hurt Sue, I knew. But I couldn't let even
her too close for fear that Kate would somehow

escape my control and say or do something that would make Sue look at me the same way that the sales assistant had looked at me the first time I met Kate, way back in '73, when she'd fallen in love with Alice's pink Christmas dress.

Poor Kate. Smothered before she'd even had a chance to live. Doomed to a lifetime in the shadows…until Helen, Alice's daughter, came out as a lesbian.

The news rocked the family. Some condemned her, most didn't care, and some – led by Sue – just loved her as if nothing had changed.

After that, Kate became restless, more vocal, and pushy. She pushed and pulled at the locks and chains I'd put on her, battering them until the creaking and groaning of my resistance nearly drove me crazy.

I escaped by attending medical conferences worldwide; Sue never accompanied me because I never asked her to. Those solitary trips away were Kate's refuge. I'd stay in a hotel far from the conference centre. Then I could buy the clothes Kate loved and wear them to the special clubs.

When I was back home, I avoided being alone with Sue; when I wasn't avoiding her, I snapped and snarled.

'What's wrong?' she asked.

'Work,' I'd say, my favourite. Or, 'Nothing.'

'Are you ill?'

'No.'

'Are you having an affair?'

'No!'

She didn't believe me. She lost weight, and, worse, Sue lost her vivaciousness. The fear that still fought to keep Kate locked away, the fear that almost destroyed me each time I resisted Kate, also began to destroy my beloved Sue.

'Tell her the truth,' Kate whispered when I lay awake, listening to Sue's subdued sobs become the soft snores I'd loved to hear for thirty years.

'She'll stop loving me.'

'Look how she loves Helen. Why won't she love you...and me?'

'I'll lose her if I tell her about you.'

'You're losing her anyway,' Kate hissed. She was right. I was losing Sue because I could no longer deny Kate.

The following day, I went downstairs to find Sue.

'Sue,' I said, and something in my voice must have alerted her, for she clumsily replaced the cordless kettle on its base and turned to me, face drawn, eyes smudged with strain and fear. 'Sue,' I said again, 'I have something to tell you ...'

I waited a year for Sue to make her decision. One long, emotional roller-coaster of a year that immolated us both on the fires of despair, of shock and uncertainty as we tried to figure out our future.

'I love you,' Sue would say on the good days. 'I married you! Our vows are for better or worse.'

'What will everyone say?' she sobbed after the initial consultation with my medical team. First, they said, comes the social transition, telling our family and friends. Next, the medical transition — the surgery, the hormones — and finally, the legal transition. All of it was too much for Sue to bear. Kate and I sobbed with her, while I cursed this man-body of mine with every atom of my woman-soul.

That winter was the worst Cape Town had had for years. Weeks of dismal grey skies, cold and damp seeping into every part of our life, the rain hammering against the windows, blurring the view of Table Mountain we'd looked at every breakfast for decades.

By the time spring came around, I was desperate for an answer from Sue. Kate had waited fifty years; she could wait no longer to be born.

        'Sue,' I said, one bright spring morning, 'where are we going?'

        'Rupert—Kate,' she said, correcting herself as she slid her hands inside my bathrobe, her fingers gently gripping the whorls of hair that would disappear when I started the hormone treatment. 'Darling Kate—let's do this.'

        'Sue?' I whispered, too afraid to hope that I hadn't lost my best friend, my soul mate, my wife, the day I'd introduced her to Kate.

        'I've loved you since the day I met you. You,' she said solemnly. 'The soul, not the body, for more than thirty years. I can't stop loving you now.'

        My relief, so deep I could only stutter a reply, 'B-b-but what … what about all the changes? You hate change! What will the boys say? And,' this last fear burst from me in a rush, 'what about our…sex life?'

        'What about it?' Sue asked, only a slight tremor in the hand resting over my heart.

        'You're…straight. You like men, not women. When I'm Kate…'

        'True,' she said and laughed the same laugh I'd fallen in love with all those years ago. 'But we'll figure that out as we go along, won't we? That and all the other changes.'

        'Sue…Sue!'

        'I know,' she said, 'it's scary, but we'll do it! We'll do all of it, whatever it takes. You — and Kate — you've lived too long in prison. It's time to set Kate free. Let's start by telling the kids.'

        'Now?' I asked.

'Now,' she said, pulling her smartphone from the pocket of her old bathrobe, a green cotton terry that had faded with age but was oh-so-familiar.

We skyped Andrew first.

'Hi, Mom,' he said. 'Hi, Dad.'

'Don't call him Dad,' Sue said and smiled at me. 'Call him Kate.'

The Cave Dweller

The day I became a cave dweller started like any other Sunday. Ma and Pa, my older sister Cecily and I went into the woods.

Most of our village went into the Old Forest for every Mother's Day picnic, a feast of bread and fruits that left us replete and happy.

Even this year, so long after that fateful picnic under the trees, I hear Ma and Pa calling, calling my name, while everyone else just eats and eats. Cecily is long gone. I can't remember her voice. But Ma and Pa — they never stop coming back to this same giant yellowwood that has stood for a thousand lifetimes. Generations of our family, and so many other families from the village and the woods, have eaten beneath it and sat in its branches.

At first, I called back, but my voice had no power because I was so young. While it has become strong, and I can now make it soar above the forest noises, it's been too long, and I've changed beyond their recognition.

The Accident happened so fast the day I lost my family. One moment, I was walking behind Ma and Pa, my only interest the bread I was eating. Cecily and her friends were all around me, laughing and chirping as girls do when dressed in their prettiest party plumage.

Then…I was trapped, the great hairy hands of a cave dweller effortlessly subduing my struggles.

Ma and Pa had warned Cecily. 'Be careful when you're in the forest, Cecily; keep an eye on your baby sister,' they said. 'You never know where the cave dwellers are.'

Cecily and I exchanged glances of disbelief. Cecily, being the oldest, always braver, risked

cocking her head in a challenge. 'You're just trying to
scare us, Ma! No one's ever seen a cave dweller
around here.'

'They exist,' Ma said, her voice sharp and
shrill. 'They exist everywhere! Every year, we hear
how more and more of them are born — their villages
are already so overcrowded, some come to live in the
woods to escape the noise!'

'They're starting to move out of their caves,
taking over our woods and our land,' Pa, always
quieter than Ma, less dominant, added.

'Imagine,' Ma, as usual, talking over Pa, said.
'Living in those dark, closed-in places. We saw a cave
dweller village once, so don't you girls go thinking
you're safe. Terrible,' she shook her head, 'it was a
terrible place — row after row, so close the air
couldn't breathe between the walls. Not a tree or a
shrub to soften the blackest of them. Just narrow
windows cut into the stone…' Ma shivered as if the
horror of what she'd seen was still fresh.

Even then, before I knew what a lifetime
trapped in a cave dweller's home was like, a shiver
wracked me. A premonition, perhaps, of my waiting
future.

'Once, as a young boy,' Pa's deep voice
soothed me as he spoke. 'I actually went inside one of
the caves.' Remembered pride in his courage
underpinned his soft words.

Cecily, a Daddy's girl if ever there was one,
fluttered around him. 'Oh, Pa,' she said, 'You're so
brave!'

Pa puffed his chest out. 'Well, it was a dare
from your Uncle Bruce,' he said. 'No one thought I'd
do it, you know. I was always the quiet one.'

'Tell us more, Pa!'

'Winter was almost here. The days started late
and cold, ending early and even colder. Food was
scarce in those days.' Pa paused, eyes gazing into the

distance of memory. Cecily and I exchanged a
conspiratorial gaze. We knew Pa loved to tell a story
— lots of dramatic pauses and lyrical phrases.

'The three of us — Bruce, Tommy and I —
had escaped Ouma's nest before everyone else was
awake. Bruce was the one who said we should go
down to the cave dwellers' village.' Another pause as
he sighed. 'We were boys heading off for a Grand
Adventure. As we crept between the rows of stone
dwellings, one dwelling had left a window wide open.
Bruce dared us to peek inside, and as I leaned in —
boom!' Pa slammed the arms of his chair so hard
Cecily and I squawked in fear before dissolving into
giggles. 'He pushed me inside.' Pa was smiling at our
enjoyment; he liked nothing better than a good
audience when he was performing.

'That day,' he continued, 'changed my life.
Afterwards, I had the courage of a cat. I could face
anything. Even,' he leaned forward to give Ma a
loving tap on her tailbone as she bustled past us,
busily preparing dinner, 'even your Ma's father!'

'Oh, Arthur, not in front of the girls!' Ma said,
brushing him away, but there was so much love in her
voice we knew how thrilled she was that, after so long
together, he still found her irresistible.

'What happened next, Pa? How did you
escape the cave dweller?' Cecily asked.

'There was no one home,' he said, smiling at
our groans of disappointment. 'That day still changed
my life! After escaping the cave dweller's house, I
went straight to your mother's as soon as possible. If I
could touch a cave dweller's chair, I could face your
Ma's father.'

We nodded solemnly. We both knew how
scary Granpa Hector was, always dressed in black,
gimlet eyes peering down at us over his colossal beak
of a nose if we made the slightest noise during the
daily prayer meetings. Neither of us had ever seen Pa

as anything other than a soft, gentle soul whose
greatest asset was not his looks or his size but his
singing voice that soared above the rest of the choir
each day.

I always heard Pa's voice first in those
terrifying early days after the cave dweller captured
me. As the hours turned into days, then into months
and years, it was Pa's voice I heard calling, calling,
giving me hope in the darkness and saving my life.

My new home was a small, barred room, a
cage, really. Once I recovered from the first shock,
life wasn't too bad with the cave dweller. But a cage,
no matter how gilded, is still a cage. Oh yes, I was
always warm and dry, handfed with healthy,
nourishing food once a day. At first, my captor — a
male, I think, although it's hard to tell them apart —
would pick me up with surprising gentleness, stroking
and petting me.

'You're my special love,' he crooned. 'You're
all I have. No one loves me. Do you love me?'

Shaking in terror every time he came close, I
couldn't answer him. I dreaded those moments when
his hands cupped me for, small as I was, I could feel
their danger. No matter how softly he stroked me,
they constantly vibrated with the power to destroy.

Soon, after the novelty wore off, he kept
mumbling about what to do with me. Terror kept me
silent, making him even more frustrated.

'Say something!' he commanded, shaking me
so hard my voice froze in my throat until, there,
beyond this cave dweller's prison, out there in the
freedom of the woods, I heard Pa's voice raised high
above the forest noises, singing a lullaby he'd sung to
Cecily and me when we were babies.

As Pa's distant voice sounded, I opened my
mouth and joined him in the chorus of the song. A
small part of me hoped Pa would hear me, but his

voice faded as he moved deeper into the forest, looking for me.

Even though he never found me, Pa saved me, for when I opened my eyes again, the cave dweller's face was softened by the tears on his cheeks and the wonder in his eyes.

'Your voice,' he whispered, stroking the back of my head with a huge thumb made gentle with a love he'd been starved of for so long. 'Your song!' he sighed, 'is the most beautiful sound in the world. Sing it again. Please. Sing it again.'

And, because I felt his pain, I felt his yearning for something lost so long ago he no longer remembered what he ached for, I let my voice soar above the sound of his tears.

I'm fully grown now, and even though I still hear Pa's voice, weakened with age and time, I haven't heard Ma's voice for months. I've lived with the cave dweller for aeons. I do not sing every day, nor every time he pleads with me. I only sing when I want to, to prove to myself that, even if I was caged, even if the cave dweller ruled every other aspect of my life, in this, I was free.

I was neither a victim nor a prisoner, even though I lived like one, and there were days when the loneliness and loss tore at my heart. But my voice, my song, my essence were mine and mine alone.

The days the cave dweller wept the hardest. I came to realise he, too, knew the same terrors as I did, that his power, his domination and his strength were not enough to heal his broken heart.

So, I sang on until the day he couldn't rise from the narrow steel bed he slept on, the one he'd moved next to my cage the day I first sang for him.

'Birdie,' he gasped, 'I shouldn't have done it. I should have set you free years ago.' He struggled to move, reaching for the door of my cage, but fell back, weak and broken.

The inexplicable bond that had grown between us tore into me. I couldn't speak; I could only raise my voice in the song he loved so much. I sang and sang until the last breath rattled through his chest, and his eyes, fixed in my direction from the first note I'd uttered, fluttered closed, and a great silence descended.

The food he'd left lasted a few days. I tried everything to break the bars of the cage, flinging myself against the bars, the locked door, until I was exhausted, until I was so weak from fear and lack of food that I could only collapse on the floor and wait for the end I'd feared so much.

Pa's distant song, quivering with the ravages of old age, reminded me that another week had passed and, once again, everyone was gathering for the Sunday picnic under the giant old yellowwood in the forest close to the village I hadn't seen for so long and would never see again.

I was going to die, and in my dream state, I heard the voices of cave dwellers outside the window. Desperate to live, to sing again, I called out. I thought my voice was too weak to be heard, but then a shadow fell over my cage. The blurred outline of a young cave dweller hung over me as I lay, weak and helpless, on the filthy floor of the cage that had been my home for so long.

'Look, Ma,' it said, opening the cage door and poking my chest with a small grubby finger. 'I think it's dead like Grandpa!'

A larger female cave dweller appeared next to it. 'Eee-yew,' it said. 'Birds are supposed to be free. Your Grandpa should never have locked the poor thing in a cage!'

I quivered with fear as she reached in and picked me up. 'It's not dead yet,' she said and stroked me with fingers as gentle as those of my captor. 'Let's give it some water and see if it can fly.'

She crooned senseless words as she dripped a nourishing mix of honey and water into my beak. I sang a single note of gratitude as she returned me to my cage: I'd come to realise even captivity was better than death, until I realised she was taking my cage outside into the forest...and she left the door of my cage wide open.

I lay there for hours, the winds of the wild ruffling my feathers, the sounds of the cave dweller and her young talking to other cave dwellers who took away a long black bag containing, I was sure, the remains of my captor, my friend. Soon, the sweetened water gave me enough strength to sit up and hop onto the lintel of the open cage door as I breathed in the scent of freedom.

As I fluttered my wings, testing their strength, I heard Pa's voice once again calling, calling my name.

'Pa,' I shouted. 'Pa, I'm coming!'

I leapt out of the cage, soaring into the air as I flew in the direction of my father's excited chatter and, free for the first time since I found my voice, I sang my song for all the forest to hear.

Where the Wind Talks

Leticia first heard the wind talking when rolling down the window to cool herself. She stared at the barren landscape until it faded into a vast expanse of nothingness.

'Don't listen to the wind, Doctor Leticia,' the driver Cleophas said, swerving to avoid a pothole in the almost non-existent road, the Jeep belching a puff of smoke. 'When the wind talks, the ancestors call us, and strange things can happen.'

She nodded, smiling at his whimsy, but after a minor struggle, the window rolled fully open. As she stuck her head out, she heard the wind whistling the most beautiful sound in the world: the same sound she'd heard as a child in the ancient Dragonsback Mountains.

Sweat rolled down her legs, soaking through her khaki cargo pants and into the cracked leather seat of the old Cherokee. Twisting in her seat, she gazed at the giant sand dunes rolling by, dotted with grey boulders and small tufts of yellowing vegetation.

How can any living creature survive out here?

Easing her legs out as much as she could in the cramped space, she saw the lightweight Salomons on her feet were no longer a shiny ebony and mocha mousse but, like the rest of her, coloured a soft reddish pink from the desert dust smothering everything in a fine layer.

Was she doing the right thing?

'Look, Doctor Leticia! The Burning Place.' Cleophas, a young man with a long, narrow face and warm eyes that were deep and dreamy, pointed to a distant mountain range looming stark and rocky on the horizon. 'The mine,' he said. 'That's where it lives.'

'Uh-huh,' Leticia nodded. After four hours in the car with him, she was used to his way of speaking.

'I learn English,' he'd said as he lifted her bag off the airport luggage carousel, 'so that one day I will be mine manager.'

His dream was not as impossible as it sounded. In the non-stop commentary since they'd left the airport, he'd told Leticia of his childhood in an isolated village along the banks of the Subiek River.

'My eyes,' Cleophas said, 'have not once seen water in that river! But my mother's mother, my memekulu, speaks of the rainstorm when she was not yet a moon maiden...haa! The blessings were so great that year we still use the water the earth saved for cooking and bathing.'

'I was the first one in my clan to complete my schooling. That is why,' Cleophas rubbed the steering wheel with pride, 'I am now a driver for The Company. One day,' he added, his sideways glance both determined and anxious, 'I'll be the mine manager.'

To Leticia, coming to this desolate land from the gold-rich Great City in the south, Cleophas's dream reminded her of her dreams. They, too, had seemed impossible. Yet here she was: a *cum laude* graduate with a Ph.D. in Geology on her way to her first job as the only woman geologist employed by The Company.

Her love affair with rocks began when she won the fishing trip argument.

'I'm eight, Daddy!' she said, her spoon tapping the side of her favourite cereal bowl, the one with the pink unicorns prancing around the outside rim, their painted hooves buried deep in a spray of wildflowers. 'Charlie and Jordie went with you when they were six.' Her spoon clattered into the bowl, a splash of milk and Frosties spilling onto the breakfast counter. 'And now Pete's going too — and he's two years younger than me!'

'You're a girl, stoopid,' her oldest brother Charlie taunted. 'Girls don't like fishing.'

'Well, I won't know whether I like it until I've tried it, won't I…stoopid!'

Charlie leaned over and pulled the ribbon loose from her ponytail. 'Who're you calling—'

'Stop it! Both of you.' Taking his glasses off and pinching the bridge of his nose, her father spoke as quietly as ever. Still, neither Leticia nor her brother misunderstood the steel in Fred's voice, settling for casting sideways glares at each other. 'Your build is too small. We carry the packs up the gorge. We pitch the tents, dig the toilets — we do everything.' Fred looked across the table at his daughter's petite build. 'You're just not strong enough. When you're bigger and stronger, you can join us.'

'We'll carry Letty, Dad,' Jordie sniggered. 'Then she can cook for us.'

'Yeth, she can wash our dishes,' Pete, following his older brothers' lead, lisped through his missing front teeth.

Leticia said nothing for the rest of the meal.

That evening, when Fred came home from work, he found Charlie's tent pitched on the front lawn, a toilet hole big enough for an elephant to fall in dug next to it, and Leticia, wearing a backpack filled with unicorns, books, and bags of crisps, keeping her three brothers at bay with a shovel.

'You took my tent,' Charlie yelled, trying to duck past the swinging shovel.

'You should've watched it better,' Leticia said. A drop of sweat from her forehead meandered down her chin. She rubbed her chin on her shoulder, her eyes not moving from her brothers, as she steadfastly guarded the territory she'd gained.

Fred knew his daughter. Looking at his wife standing on the stoep watching their children, her green-and-white apron speckled with cookie dough and raised his left eyebrow in a silent query. At her slight nod, he stepped forward into the fray.

'Enough,' he said, gently removing the shovel from Letty's shaking arms, so thin and dainty he could only marvel at the strength of will that had won her argument. 'Letty, I'll take you to buy your tent tomorrow.'

'Daddy!' Leticia's elated cry echoed her brothers' protesting yelp of 'Dad!'

'Do you mean it, Daddy? I can come with you on the fishing trip?'

He nodded. 'First, fill that hole, then take down your brother's tent.'

'Fred, she's had a big day, and she's only a little —' As the protest burst from her, Fred looked at Clara, as blonde and slender as their daughter. She stood watching them, and Fred knew that next to him and the boys, who, even though young, were already showing signs of topping his six-foot height, Letty looked even smaller than she was.

'I'll do it, Mama!' Leticia said before he could reply.

Snatching the shovel back from her father, Leticia began filling in the hole she'd dug earlier with a ferocity that silenced even her brothers. 'There,' she said when the hole was filled, 'You can have it now.' A fire was lit in her when she saw the pride on her father's face and the growing respect in her brothers' eyes.

'It's my tent,' Charlie said. 'I'll help you take it down.'

'I don't need help,' she said.

'I'm not helping you, stoopid,' Charlie said, 'I'm looking after my tent in case you tear it.'

Even through her exhaustion, Leticia heard her brother's unspoken promise that she'd never be left behind again.

They were right, though, her brothers and her father. She didn't like fishing. The live worms wriggling painfully on the hooks, the beautiful iridescent trout flashing through the waters fighting to save its life, yet being dragged ever closer to the net that would finally defeat it, was all too much for her.

While they fished in Old Woman's stream, she rock-hopped over the boulders lining the edge of the clear waters. On the last day, as the sun began slipping behind Monk's Cowl peak and the first hint of the night chill crept into the wind, Leticia saw a glistening in the water.

'Look, Dad! Charlie!' she shouted, ignoring the strict instructions that any noise would scare off the fish rising to catch the late afternoon peak of insects skimming the water. 'I've found a diamond!'

Before they'd even lifted their heads, Leticia plunged into the pool. A strong swimmer, she was unafraid of the small but deep pool; she never heard the frantic sound of Fred dropping his rod and cursing as, hampered by his heavy wading boots, he was too slow to stop her diving in. All Leticia heard was the music of the stone, calling, calling to her to find it, to save it from the depths of the water so that its beauty could catch the dying rays of the sun and send them shooting out into the world as it glinted in her hand.

Under the water, she sank, unerringly knowing where the glittering stone lay. The water distortion meant nothing. She was not using her eyes to find the stone calling her, for a subtle vibration radiating from the stone guided her unerringly to the bottom of the pool.

With the minimum amount of scratching, she pried her treasure loose from the mud and slime. Clutching it tightly in her hand, she thrust upward, bursting through the pool surface with her prize triumphantly held aloft just as Fred plunged in to save her.

'Woo-hoo!' she shouted over their bellows of relief, young Pete's panicked sobbing dwindling into hiccups as he heard his sister's voice. 'I got it! I rescued my diamond!'

'That's not a diamond,' Fred said, angry relief making him bundle her so quickly out of the pool she yelped as her knee scraped against a rough boulder jutting out of the edge of the pool where Charlie and Jordie lay, arms stretched out to grab her to safety. 'That's just quartz. You could have been drowned, all for a common quartz!'

Not even her father's irritable identification of her treasure nor the brusque drying her brothers gave her as she shivered in the afternoon shadows could dim Leticia's fascination with the quartz. Tingling in her hand, the clear quartz spread its warmth outward, running up her arm into her heart, decanting magic into her blood. She knew then that she could see and feel something in the rocks that no one else could. She could hear them whisper as if they were living creatures.

Looking back, she always knew her dream, her soul's mission, was born in the ancient Dragonsback Mountains that afternoon. An afternoon that could so easily have ended in tragedy.

She still carried that small quartz with her wherever she went, from her first day at school to her last day of university, as she walked across the stage in the red gown of a Doctor of Geological and Mineralogical Sciences.

She'd rubbed it between her fingers as, a day before her final exam, she heard the news that her mother had died of a sudden heart attack. The professor and her fellow students — all male — had rallied around her.

'You've had a terrible shock, Letty,' they consoled. 'No one will expect you to get that cum laude anymore.'

'If you need a special dispensation to delay your finals, my girl,' her professor said, patting her clumsily on her shoulder. 'I'll arrange one.'

Hidden in the pocket of her jeans, her fingers rubbed her quartz. The crystal started to vibrate gently, a warmth creeping up her veins into her frozen heart until she heard Clara whisper, '*You're stronger than this, Letty. You have more choice than I did.* '

She shook her head to clear the voice and the sudden wetness in her eyes, but her mother's voice was insistent. '*Don't listen to them. This is* your *dream, Letty. You can't give up now.*'

'The funeral is next week,' she said to the professor. 'I'll still be able to write the exam tomorrow.' Leticia smiled faintly at the look of dismay on the professor's face as he imagined his funding being lost because his star pupil hadn't performed as expected.

'*Good girl, Letty!*' she imagined Clara saying.

Before she flipped the question paper over the following day, she rubbed her special quartz between her fingers. Then, carefully placing the quartz on the edge of the desk, she took a deep breath and began to write.

Weeks later, when her mother's funeral was long over, an envelope from the university arrived. She stood looking at the logo, only the slight tremble in her fingers revealing her anxiety.

'Open it, Letty,' her father said in that strange new voice he had since he'd lost Clara, the voice that made her grief simmer hot and threaten to boil over. 'The results won't change no matter how long you look at it.'

'They won't,' she agreed and ripped the envelope open, fumbling with the single sheet of paper, her throat working as she read.

Fred leaned forward, the cream leather of his La-Z-Boy armchair squeaking in protest as he clicked it back into an upright position. 'You didn't pass the degree cum laude?'

'No,' she said.

'Don't worry; a pass is good enough under the circumstances.'

'No,' she said again and, hearing a whisper of her mother's laugh, swallowed hard on the tears.

'You didn't pass at all?' He stood up, wanting to hug her, but that had been Clara's department, so he touched her arm gently instead.

'Not cum laude, Dad,' she said. 'I passed summa cum laude!'

'I knew you could do it, Letty!' she heard Clara say. *'You can do anything!'*

Now here she was, her mousy blonde hair blowing loose from its ponytail, her face gritty from the fine red sand whipped up by the wind in the middle of one of the world's oldest deserts, the ubiquitous dunes shifting even as she watched the austere landscape, exactly replicating her teenage imagining of the planet Arrakis in her favourite novel *Dune*. Her heart, happier than it had been in years, leapt at the thought of what rocks she'd find in these sands tomorrow.

She was on her way to a prestigious job where, even considering the small village that

Cleophas came from, she was the only woman in fifty clicks. This was her impossible dream come true, and Cleophas, too, had what to others was an impossible dream.

'My dream came true, Cleophas,' she said. 'You'll be mine manager one day.'

He burst into a smile, then pointed ahead with his chin. 'Look, Miss,' he said, 'There's the offices.'

Leticia drew her head back in the car window. Closing the window with a little shake of her head, she dismissed the feeling that she'd just experienced another moment like when she first saw her lucky quartz crystal glinting in the mountain riverbed.

Looking forward to where Cleophas was pointing, Leticia saw nothing but kilometres of red sand leading up to a mountain range, a few scrappy grey-green bushes and a crop of bizarre succulents, their burnt and split leaves fat with stored water, meandering wildly amongst yellowing tufts of grass. Then her gaze adjusted, and a collection of ramshackle buildings leapt out of the heat haze.

Cleophas sped through the security gate with a spin worthy of an F1 driver and drew the Jeep to a halt in front of the largest building. The russet brick structure was double-storied, with a row of offices in front of the enormous washing plant. Moaning conveyor belts hungrily fed the mill uncrushed gravel scooped out of the ancient riverbed, half covered with the shifting red sands. Grey gravel hills were scattered across to the left, those great piles of uncrushed rock residue spat out by the crushing plant. To the right, tucked against the mountain for some relief, however slight, from the implacable heat of the desert sun and far enough away from the offices and crushing plant to provide some noise reduction, was the living compound that would be her home for the next few years.

'You are here,' said Cleophas said. 'I will take you to the boss.'

Leticia's palms itched with grime from the journey and a sudden moistness. She'd had to prove herself to her father and brothers in her childhood and to her professors and fellow geology students year after year during her studies. In this isolated complex, walking down a passage lined with stern-faced men from bygone eras looking down on her as she wiped her palms on her khaki trousers, what chance that equality and feminism had already found a home here?

As the old sepia tones turning large black moustaches into a dirty red — or perhaps that was simply a patina of the dust she could already tell was part of life here at the Daureb Mine — segued into photos of modern mine managers, Leticia heard an argument from behind the door that stood ajar at the end of the passageway.

'Ai! Ai! Ai!' said Cleophas. 'That Piet! He's an old man but with a child spirit.'

'Why are we getting this woman?' a heavily accented voice demanded. 'This'll be nothing but trouble, Meneer!'

As Cleophas raised his hand to knock on the door, announcing their arrival, Leticia clutched his wrist, stopping him with a finger over her mouth. She would handle this as she'd handled every other challenge in her life: head-on. From Cleophas's wicked grin of conspiracy as he dropped his hand, she knew she had at least one friend here.

'Rubbish, Piet,' said a younger voice. 'How long have we been trying to get someone of that calibre to work here? Leticia Calder was consistently at the top of the national exam results. She's the best of the new crop of geologists, and she's a PhD.'

'But…she's a woman, boss!'

'She's willing to do the work, Piet! Nobody else wants to work here. We're too remote, and the bloody local hauntings chase everyone off. We're lucky to have her.'

'She's a single woman, Meneer.'

'So is my daughter.'

'But…this one is coming to work here! With all us men!

'And the problem is…?'

'If you put her in a mine house…all those spare rooms.' Piet's voice was awkward but stoical in his determination to convey his indignation. 'What's she going to get up to?'

'Are you befok, Piet? Are you suggesting she'll start a *brothel*?'

The younger voice — the mine manager's, Leticia assumed — had a sharp edge. Time to let them know she had arrived. With a quick glance at Cleophas, propping up the passage wall, his eyes calmly watching her, Leticia put her hand in her pocket to rub her lucky quartz, then took a deep breath and pushed the door open.

One man, with pale brown hair and, behind a pair of horn-rimmed spectacles, angry brown eyes, was in his late thirties, young compared to the other man but old enough to be a mine manager. Of medium height, he stood behind an enormous mahogany desk which, if the nicks and dents in the surface were an indication, had served all the previous mine managers in the photos lining the passage. Dressed in khaki cargo pants, not too dissimilar to those she wore, with an open-necked blue cotton shirt rolled up to the elbows, he looked relaxed and calm despite his downward curving mouth and tightened lips.

In front of the desk stood a man in his mid-fifties, dressed in a checked linen safari suit, a black comb sticking jauntily out the top of his beige knee-high socks in defiance of the sternly fastened laces of his suede Grasshopper veldskoens.

'Which of you is Piet?' she asked, knowing full well which of the two he was.

'That's me,' he said, his shoulders jerking back.

Leticia's petite stature was a disadvantage. She pulled herself up as high as she could, stretching her arm to rest her hand on his chest, just above his paunch, hanging heavy over his belt as a testament to his loving attachment to too many beers.

'Piet,' she said sugary sweet, feeling his old heart give a terrified leap. 'I can promise you this: even if I did start a brothel, you wouldn't be able to afford my prices. Don't worry too much, you're safe.' She gave his chest one more pat, smiling as he removed a crumpled white handkerchief from one of the many pockets on his safari suit to wipe away sweat beading on his forehead.

'It's hot in here,' Piet said when he saw she'd noticed. He pointed to the open window and added, 'The boss doesn't like air conditioning.'

Turning to the grinning man behind the desk, she asked, 'Are you Gerry Barlow?'

'I am,' he said, standing up and stretching a firm hand over the desk. 'Welcome to the Daureb. Don't believe Piet,' he added, sweeping a sly glance at the older man. 'We're a friendly bunch, and you're a much-needed team member.' He looked at his watch, a durable Casio G-Shock she'd once admired until, for her PhD graduation, her father and brothers had clubbed together to buy her the stainless steel Tag Heuer F1 she wore. 'There's time before sundowners for me to show you around the compound. Cleophas!'

'Mr Gerry?' Cleophas said, his carefully blank face belied by the wise amusement in his eyes as he took in the representation of the past, present, and

future standing before him in the shape of these three
different people.

'Take Dr Calder's baggage to unit eight and
leave the keys in the door.'

'Yes, Mr Gerry.' Although Cleophas didn't
quite salute, there was respect and liking in his
response, telling Leticia that Gerry Barlow might be
another ally.

'That's a young man who is going to go far,'
Gerry said, flicking two bright red hard hats off a
wooden stand by the door and handing one to Leticia.
'He's smart, hard-working, and nothing ever upsets
him.' Ushering Leticia past all those old photographs,
which, she now thought, looked less disapproving,
and out into the blinding sun, Gerry added, 'Let's start
with the washing plant first, then head for the pit
before I show you around the new accommodation.'

'New accommodation?' Leticia asked, looking
in the direction of the housing compound, where the
rows of cool white housing units were shaded a desert
red, the once-green tin roofs a dirty grey, and the
single garage attached to each unit nothing but a
ramshackle lean-to buckling under the weight of the
sand creeping up the pre-fab walls.

'We've only been in this location for about
fifty years. Local legend says there's an old town
swallowed up by the desert. Mainly,' Gerry laughed,
'the legend is repeated in the months we don't meet
tonnage. The excuse is that the old town is where the
main vein is, but the ancestors buried it when the
commercial miners got greedy and started excavating
too much, too quickly.'

'What is the daily tonnage here at the
Daureb?' Leticia asked as they walked towards the
working pit past a high, fifteen-strand barbed wire
fence strung along wooden timber posts bleached pale
by the relentless sun. Behind the fence, the skeletal
blue arms of an on-site crusher, like a dying man

grasping for a drop of water, reached for the sky over the pit's edge. A large yellow sign in several languages, including English, proclaiming MINING AREA | NO UNAUTHORISED ENTRY |TRESPASSERS WILL BE PROSECUTED, hung loosely off one fence post, clattering in the ever-present wind whipping the loose sand from the graded road, stinging her face and making her grateful she'd slipped on the wide framed-dark glasses protecting her eyes as they'd left the office building.

'We excavate about 100 tons per hour of Kimberlite for stage crushing and sluicing, and then…' His voice faded in the noise of ore and gravel being crushed and then spewed out onto the long conveyor belts carrying it to the roll-crusher, pulverising it into smaller pieces on its way to being scrubbed and separated for recovery.

Leticia, pausing to wipe the sweat trickling out from under her hard hat, looked at the scene before her: the men and the machinery fuzzy in the heat haze, the insufferable noise — she must bring her earplugs with her the next time she visited the plant, another reason why she preferred being a geologist, more often than not it was just her, the immense wilderness she was enticing to give up its treasures and silence — and, looming over it all, the grim rocky mountain that was both the source of their work and their only protection against the persistent wind and sand.

'Bleak; isn't it?' Gerry said.

'Yes,' she said, shivering as the wind blew chill over her arms despite the day's heat, murmuring and moaning. 'But beautiful in its own way,' she added, shivering again as the wind fell silent as if calmed by her praise. Following Gerry as he headed to the site manager's office, she thought how easy it would be for the wind and the sand to swallow up a whole town so that it disappeared, never to be found again.

Within a day, Leticia had her bearings and a working routine. Early each morning, before the sun rose to scorch the few tufts of grass struggling for survival in the sand-encrusted slopes of the mountain, she'd head out on foot, compass in one hand, water, food, and the fully charged transportable VT1 in her backpack, her portable hand tools lashed on top, and her lucky quartz crystal safely tucked into a zipped pocket. Any significant discovery, she told Gerry, she'd mark the coordinates and return to the compound to plan a proper excavation.

The best part of her day was sitting in the dark before dawn, pouring her first cup of coffee from the flask, dunking a buttermilk rusk fresh baked in the mine's canteen. Sitting there, her legs hanging over the edge of Orion's pass, the narrow footpath leading up into the mountains from behind the pit manager's office, she could hear them whispering, those crystals she was sure were buried deep in the heart of the inhospitable peaks looming over the desert ocean surrounding them. She could hear them just as she'd heard the call of her lucky quartz that had lain lost and drowned for aeons in the Old Woman's Stream high in the Dragonsback Mountains, where her father and brothers had taken her on her first fishing trip.

In that water-rich range, the quartz had gurgled and bubbled its way into her soul; here, the gemstones talked to her in the whispers of the wind.

Listening to the wind talk made her first month on the Daureb bearable. Piet's discontent at her presence in the mine compound spread to the other men. As she walked into the canteen, conversations would halt for a second. Even those men she worked well with during the searing afternoon planning sessions would dip their heads, fascinated by the meat and veg on their dinner plates, avoiding eye contact. Only Gerry was utterly relaxed around her.

'What's up with the guys this time, Gerry?' she asked, sliding onto the bench beside him where he, isolated by his status and language, always sat alone. 'Surely they can't all think like Piet?'

Gerry grinned. 'They're worried about the showers at the pit.'

'What?' she choked, halfway between amusement and annoyance. '*I'm* more likely to be spied on than they are! I'm the only woman — and I shower in the guest changeroom two units away.'

'What can I say?' Gerry shrugged. 'The heat and the sand make us all imagine crazy things.'

Leticia carefully placed her knife and fork together, her lips compressing as she sat back and looked around the canteen. She'd never felt more isolated, not even in her first months at university. At least there, she'd lived in a female dormitory and had made a few friends who, like her, had wanted to do more with their degree than use it as a route to find a trust fund husband. Over copious bottles of cheap red wine, they'd laughed and cried and made plans to work hard enough to prove themselves equal to any challenge they faced.

Would this game never end?

Sighing with exhaustion, she stood up, muttering, 'Good night, Gerry.' Leaving the canteen with her head down so she didn't have to make eye contact with any of the closed-off faces of her colleagues, she turned left, heading for her unit. The hot desert air was nosediving into the night cold. As she paused to zip her parka, she thought, *this prejudice is like a mosquito: I must kill it immediately. If I wait and hope it disappears, I'll be bled dry by a million irritating bites.* And she shivered as a sudden gust of wind scurried around her

ankles, rustling the sand with approval at her decision
to act.

The next day, at the end of another day of
brutal sun and heat, her khakis damp with sweat and
dirt, her boots permanently reddish pink from the
pervasive sand, her hair clammy and plastered to her
head by her hard hat, she felt toughened by an ancient
strength absorbed during the hours of slow digging
among gravel-filled crevices and dried-up riverbeds.
Packing up her tools for the day and checking her
compass before she started the trek back to the mine
compound, her hands still hummed, vibrating with the
sense of something precious buried close to where she
worked.

As she crested Orion's Pass, the highest point
of the mountain path leading to and from the back of
the mine pit, she paused to adjust the hip straps of her
pack. On the peak of a dune in the distance, a single
oryx walked with stately ease across the top of the
shifting sand, its unmistakable rapier horns and
compact, muscular body silhouetted against the
setting sun.

Breathing in the beauty of the dying desert
day, her face cooled quickly under the breeze laden
with the sharp, bitter scent of the peculiar !kharos
plant. She'd first seen the meandering succulent that
had evolved out of the Jurassic age, miraculously
surviving for thousands of years in the arid
environment, on the day she arrived.

Since then, she'd come to know the desert was
far from lifeless sand and searing sun: from the rare
sighting of the desert lion to the squeaks and clicks
heralding the appearance of the nocturnal sand gecko,
the stark contrasts of this mysterious land unfurled a
passion in her soul. Her jaw tightened as she jerked
the buckle of the hip straps tighter. *No one,* she

thought, *was going to chase her away from her dream
life.*

The dusk was deep when she reached the
ablution blocks built inside the pit fence. Cleophas, in
his usual after-hours blue jeans and t-shirt, was
leaning against the Cherokee.

'*Halau*, Doc,' he said. 'Did you find them
yet?'

'Not yet,' she said. 'I'm feeling them closer
every day.' Unlike the other men, who would sneer
and scorn such a statement, Cleophas gave a quick
double-clap, grinning widely.

'The time will come when they call you.'

She exhaled deeply, the whoosh of her breath
strengthening her courage. 'What would you do,
Cleophas,' she asked, 'If your dream was in danger
because of someone else?'

He knew what she was talking about, for his
gaze flicked quickly at the brightly lit ablution block
where men's voices speculated loudly on what dinner
would be and who would win the weekend's rugby
national cup, and then back to where she stood,
lowering her pack to the ground and rotating her
shoulders to loosen the tension.

'What are you going to do, Doc?'

'Watch and learn, Cleophas,' she said and
rubbed her lucky quartz before pushing up her shirt
sleeves. 'Watch and learn.'

Leaving him laughing behind her, she reached
the door in three giant strides, slamming the door
open with such force that the raucous chatter of
machismo died instantly. Hoping they wouldn't see
her heart fluttering wildly beneath her ribcage, she
walked past each of them as if she were a Queen
inspecting a military parade.

Approaching the end of the row of mullet-faced men, she asked, 'Is that all you've got to show me? I've seen better, so,' she crossed her arms across her chest and sneered. 'You can all relax because I don't want or need what you can offer.'

The stunned silence behind her as she turned quickly changed. As she stepped back into the night, she heard the first shout of deep laughter. By the time she reached the Cherokee, Andries, a young mining engineer who'd arrived at the Daureb a couple of days after her, came rushing out.

'You got us *lekker*, hey!' he shouted, punching the air with a muscular hand, the other holding tightly onto the damp towel now wrapped around his waist. '*Nou's jy een van die manne!*'

As if I want to be one of the men! Leticia laughed anyway, giving him a quick thumbs-up.

Cleophas, still leaning against the Cherokee, touched her shoulder lightly. 'They'll never really understand, Doc,' he said, his voice soft with understanding. 'My memekulu says they mean no harm; it is what their ancestors taught them.'

'Your grandmother is wise,' she said, a quick smile easing the tiredness from her jaw. 'Night, Cleophas,' she added, crossing the smooth dust of the recently graded road and heading for the peace of her unit. Taking a cool beer from the small gas fridge each unit was provided with, she opened the window, where she could sense more than see the looming mountain. Breathing in the desert air, she said aloud, 'There. That's sorted,' and the mountain hummed as a gust of wind swept over the pit and through the housing compound.

True to Andries's word, the men lost their reserve around her after the Ablution Ambush.

'Hey, Letty, join us for a dop!' they'd shout as she walked through the door of the Desert Rose.

From the outside, the Desert Rose was just another pre-fab unit. Once inside, the bleached oryx skull mounted on the wall, its spear horns so long they almost touched the creosoted timber struts in the thatched ceiling, the rows of booze bottles glinting in the low-lit mirror behind the timber counter that Cleophas manned with aplomb and the smell of smoke, stale beer and sweat filling the air as Sade oozed smoothly out of the jukebox made the Desert Rose akin to the smoky, beer-scented Roxy Bar in Melville, a favourite haunt of her undergrad days.

Cleophas would wink and slam a bottle of vodka on the countertop; she'd drink from that all night, aware that she had their acceptance but not their respect.

Until she found the pod.

From the day of her arrival, she'd felt a special crystal calling, something otherworldly out there in the heat-ravaged heart of the mountain.

Every day, she set out before dawn, up over Orion's Pass and down into the belly of the domed-shaped mountain range, searching for the source of the whisper that came to her on the breath of the wind. Sometimes, it called with a soft breeze; other times, it howled like a wild witch cackling on a broomstick.

Every evening, Cleophas waited at the pit gate when she returned from her explorations.

'Nothing today, Doc?' he'd ask, assessing her with those wise brown eyes.

She shook her head. 'I know there's something out there, Cleophas! I'm looking in the wrong places.'

'Carry on listening, Doc,' he'd say, 'The wind will tell you what it wants to.'

The way he spoke lifted the hair in the nape of her neck.

'What do you know you're not telling me, Cleophas?'

'I hear what you hear, Doc,' he'd laugh, then head off to the Desert Rose for his bartender duties.

She'd never get anything more from him, but there was something numinous about the way he spoke, the way he watched her, and the way he was everywhere. He knew everyone, and everyone knew Cleophas.

'What's with Cleophas?' she asked Gerry after their weekly meeting.

'He's our good luck. Our mascot.' Gerry leaned his chair back, the brown leather creaking with age and heat. 'When I took over from Stefaan Bosman as manager, he told me if Cleophas is ill, no one will work. If Cleophas leaves the mine, the locals all leave.' Gerry rolled his shoulders and sat forward. 'His grandmother is one of the ancients in the clan. At best estimate, she's about one hundred and two, so I guess it's respect or superstition.'

Leticia started gifting Cleophas with something small she found in the mountains for his grandmother. A piece of sun-bleached deadwood that looked like a porcupine. A small heart-shaped stone sandblasted into smoothness over centuries. A fossilised fragment of shell from a large bird's egg.

'You understand the soul of this land, Doc,' he said, rubbing a reverent finger over the fossil. 'Only those the wind talks to can find these treasures.'

As the early morning summer fog they called the malmokkies no longer rolled in from the west with its life-giving dew, transforming into the gale-force sandstorms of winter, Leticia watched and waited and walked the unpredictable mountains, no longer looking but listening.

On a moonlit night, she lay awake listening to the wind whistling through the compound. A loose flap of corrugated iron on the roof clattered with each gust until she could stand it no more. Flinging back the light cotton sheet, she shrugged her windbreaker over her pyjamas, knowing the night temperatures were dropping rapidly, and slipped her sockless feet into her boots to avoid being stung by a scorpion. Grabbing her torch, she followed the sound, head down against the wind. As she glanced up to gain her bearings, there beyond the pit, rising from the centre of the mountains, the sky was ablaze with an eerie radiance, enchanting her with ribbons of yellow, red, and orange leaping through the sky to kiss the Milky Way.

She stood for aeons, perhaps only minutes, watching the light burn and dim, listening to a delicate susurration of voices chanting on the wind. Deep within her, a knowing arose: this golden light would change her life. As she watched the ebb and flow shift endlessly from deep amber to brilliant yellow and back again, she was in such rapture that when a hand touched her arm, she gasped in shock.

'Are you ok?' Gerry asked.

'I'm fine,' she replied. 'Did you hear it too?'

'I heard you close your door,' he said.

'I came out to find the roof that was banging, and I saw that,' Leticia said, pointing to the blazing sky.

'Saw what?' asked Gerry.

When Leticia turned back, the desert was dark again, and the wind was silent. A light breeze ruffled a few tendrils that had come loose from the thick plait she bound her hair into each night before going to bed.

'There was an aurora, Gerry, the most beautiful glow illuminating the desert sky.'

'Oh,' said Gerry, and grinned. 'You either had too much vodka at the Desert Rose tonight, or you've seen the hauntings.'

She knew it wasn't too much vodka. 'The hauntings?' she asked.

'The local people say only the chosen ones can hear the wind talk. It's nonsense, of course – only a legend. I've been here five years, and I've never seen or heard anything. What did you see?'

'I don't know what I saw,' Leticia said, a spring of excitement coiling tightly in her belly. She knew what she had seen. She also knew his masculine pragmatism wouldn't let him believe her. 'The moonrise, I think.'

'Let me walk you back to your unit,' Gerry offered.

'I'll stay out for a while longer,' she said. 'The sky is beautiful tonight.'

'Be alert,' Gerry said. 'Andries reported what could be lion spoor to the northwest of the pit yesterday.'

'Do they roam this far into the sand desert?'

'Not usually, but you never know in this place,' he said, hunching his shoulders against the cold and tucking his hands in his pockets. 'Good night.'

'Good night,' she replied. She sat on the ground, resting her back against a fence post, her gaze already on the mountain, waiting for the wind to talk to her again.

She lost track of time, falling into a light doze until she jerked awake, a fleeting fear freezing her throat. Her night vision adjusted rapidly in the light of the full moon. 'Cleophas,' she said, letting her head fall back against the fence pole, her sleepy gaze roaming over him. 'You look…different.'

He looked imposing, wearing a traditional loincloth made of animal hide and a full kaross cloaking his shoulders against the cool winter night. He wore an intricately woven headband of blue and white beads adorned with small straight horns that looked to Leticia as if they came from a petite steenbok long dead. His necklace was crafted from broken pieces of ostrich egg and slung across his back was a wooden bow and an old hide quiver filled with arrows.

His face was still the face of the young man she'd first met at the airport. His eyes, though, were different. They had deepened into dark pools of ancient mystery, wisdom swirling in their depths as if he alone carried the history of a thousand generations of his people's sorrow and joy, hope and despair, kindness and rugged toughness that could endure all the trials the gods tested them with.

'*Is* there a lion around?' she asked, pointing to the weapons he carried.

'Under the calabash moon, the chosen ones hunt another treasure,' he said and nodded towards the mountain.

She jumped to her feet and clasped his arm as he did a quick shuffle and hop to channel her excitement. 'Did you see the burning place too, Cleophas? Did you? I thought I'd imagined it!'

'The hauntings are real, Letty. But you must be quick to find what you seek. There are only a few hours before dawn breaks, and the calabash moon comes but once a year.'

She was already at her gate before he'd finished speaking, hurriedly changing into her work gear and gathering her equipment, shoving her tools, water supplies, and food into the bag, checking that her VT1 was fully charged, hooking it to her belt and safely zipping her lucky quartz into a pocket on her trousers before running back to join Cleophas where he stood silently observing the mountain. The golden aurora was back, and as she calmed her jagged breathing, she heard it again: a multitude of voices carried on the light breeze that had sprung up.

'Will you remember where it is?'

She nodded, hitching her pack into a secure position on her shoulders. 'I'm ready.'

'Come then, I will walk you to the pit gate, but you must go through Orion's Pass alone.'

Her chin lifted. 'Not a problem, I've walked it so many times already I can follow that route blindfolded.'

They didn't speak again until they reached the wire gate leading from the pit to the mountain path; Cleophas was lost in his thoughts while Leticia focused all her energy on memorising the location of the burning place as best she could.

'*!Gâi!gâb.*' He wished her good luck as he unlocked the gate with the key he took from a small pocket sewn onto his hunting quiver.

'*Gangans.*' Thanking him in his language, she added, 'How do I thank…' she nodded to the golden light stream dancing in the distance. '…them? The hauntings?'

'You'll find a way, Letty. Go now. The sun is coming soon.'

She walked briskly to Orion's Pass without looking back. She knew he would be watching her and that, however long it took, he would still be waiting when she returned.

Once through the pass, Leticia walked as fast as she could, heading towards the Bain Gorge in the northwestern periphery of the mountain, where the burning flares were brightest. The wind shifted, and murmuring voices echoed through the night, disorientating her so that she wandered off the narrow track. A fiery sensation, sudden and sharp, ran along her right thigh. Thinking it might be a scorpion she'd disturbed clambering through an outcropping of rocks to follow the pulsing sky, she scrambled out of her khakis. The intense pain disappeared, only to return immediately as she pulled her trousers up.

'Oh, it's you,' she said, slapping the pocket where her lucky crystal rested and laughing, the sound bouncing off the towering granite mountain ridges surrounding her. Removing her lucky quartz, she was unsurprised, in this mystical place, to find it was no longer a cold, clear white but aflame with the same golden red of the burning place she was heading for.

'Is this where you came from? How did you find your way to the Dragonsback Mountains? And how many million years ago did you get lost?' she asked, tenderly rubbing the crystal between her palms until it purred. 'Can you show me the way back to your home?'

There was no answer from the quartz except for a deepening of its colour. Clutching it in her hand like a Brunton's compass, Leticia let the changing warmth and colour of the quartz guide her unerringly closer to the burning place until, as the dawn's blush chased away the last of the night's shadows, she stumbled on the first ring of burnt rock.

In her months of wandering this dome-like wasteland, she'd still come to expect a few hardy !kharos succulents and a few tufts of tough grass scattered on the red-rocked slopes. This ring, about three meters wide, and she didn't yet know how deep, was devoid of vegetation, the black rock shimmering in the rising sun as if a million multicoloured stars were scattered in its heart.

'This is it,' she said aloud, sliding the heavy pack off her back. 'This is the burning place.' She cocked her head, intimidated by the unusually silent grandeur surrounding her. There was no wind, not even a breath of air, and even the haunting voices she'd heard on the wind didn't answer her.

With a click of her tongue to chase away her fancies, she slipped her lucky quartz, now cold as rock should be, back into her pocket and drank from her water bottle before unhooking her rock pick from its holster on her belt.

Scratching the black, clinker-like rock surface, she saw a flash of purple: with a practiced swing of her pick, she split open the rock. A single amethyst point set in a clear quartz cluster on a matrix of the burnt rock tumbled into her waiting hand. Holding the specimen up to the sun, she gasped at the perfect clarity of the clear quartz and the royal purple richness of the amethyst, with its tantalising glimpse of a visible enhydro bubble running the length of the point. The strength of the hum stemming from the crystal made her dizzy and confused, as if the vastness of the night sky she'd walked under to reach this unearthly place, as silent as it was bare, had scrambled her senses, making her an alien in this desert wilderness she yearned to call home.

As Leticia cupped the unique crystal, she knew then that this was what she'd searched for since she was six, fighting to join her father and brothers on their fishing trip in the Dragonsback Mountains. Wiping the sweat off her forehead, she sat back on her haunches. Her gaze followed the line of black rock, noticing sea green prehnite, amethysts, the clearest quartz, and even, she guessed, some diamonds, all sparkling in the morning sun.

Unable to resist their seductive beauty, Leticia started crawling along the ground, chasing the black vein, cracking open a pod here, loosening a rough stone there, losing track of distance and time as she crooned words of praise and appreciation for each beauty she found, her hands trembling with joy, her vision blurring from the brilliance of the colours, the heat of the rising sun combining with the power of the crystals, until she was so thirsty she forced herself to stand, looking back at where she'd left her backpack, with her water and the rest of her equipment.

As she stood, a wave of dizziness swamped her. Vivid shades of yellow engulfed her, sucking her into a vortex so that she clutched her arms around her head, protecting her face from the rocks tumbling around her and from the weird, elongated faces throbbing inside her head, mouths agape, almond-shaped eyes hollow and green, the same sea-green of the prehnite quartz cradled in the black ring of rock she'd been following. They called and called to her for help, but she hardly heard them over the sound of the screaming and the heat, the burning, burning inferno that blasted the faces and her consciousness into oblivion.

When Leticia woke, her head throbbing, she was unsure if seconds or hours had passed. At first, she thought she was still hallucinating from carelessly allowing herself to become dehydrated in the fierce desert heat. She lay at the bottom of a deep gully, crunched up against a rock half blocking the entrance to a cave. The mouth of the cave had been widened to form an old mine shaft, and the faint, welcoming sound of an underground stream trickled from the belly of the cave.

Before her, about thirty meters from the cave, lay a surreal tableau of dilapidated houses: remnants of brightly coloured paint peeled off walls, rolling banks of sand burst through abandoned doors and porches, and a rusted iron sign, pronouncing SPERRGEBIET | RESTRICTED ZONE clanged lazily in the falling wind.

This must be the ghost town. Leticia rubbed her jaw to ease her jarred teeth, her tongue rolling around a loosened molar. *This is where the hauntings awaken.*

She gazed reflectively at the old town, wondering what was hidden beneath the encroaching sand, what stories each broken house could tell of those long-dead miners who had lived and loved within their walls. 'No,' she told herself sternly, resisting the urge to explore. 'I need water first.'

Pushing against the mound of desert sand that had stopped her fall, she shuffled upright, pausing to let a residual dizziness fade. Searching for a severe injury, she ran her hands over her aching body. *Nothing broken*, she thought with relief. *Mostly bruises and some cuts.* Then, her fingers found a torn flap of fabric. 'My lucky quartz,' she exclaimed, dismayed to find the pocket ripped open, her quartz lost during her fall.

Leticia felt a sob, half fear, half exhaustion, claw dangerously against her chest. *What will I do without my lucky quartz?* She stopped her rising panic by stumbling into the cool of the underground cave in search of the stream she'd heard dribbling through the black rock walls.

Expecting, in the cool darkness, to find the stream by following the sound of the seeping water, she was astonished at how much light there was inside the cave. Flickering brightly in the far corner, an old miner's lamp lay half-submerged in an underground pool fed by water seeping through the black rock. The lamp's warm yellow light shimmered off the cave walls, infusing an eerie sense of movement into the primitive red ochre paintings of dancing tribesmen sacrificing a sacred oryx before a trio of elongated figures with almond-shaped green eyes set in gaunt triangular faces.

Towering over the tiny tribesmen, the figures stood in a doorway, painted over a large fissure in the cave wall, leading the tall men from a saucer-shaped full moon, burning with a fiery red-orange that scorched the earth around it. Each of the three strange figures held a calabash, flaming the same celestial yellow as the half-submerged miner's lamp.

How is that lamp still burning in the water? Leticia winced as she eased herself down on one knee to drink thirstily from the pool. Her cupped hand froze halfway to her mouth, the precious liquid running down her arm before soaking her shirt as she saw the light didn't come from a lamp but — if she wasn't mistaken — if she wasn't still hallucinating from dehydration — if the distinct octahedral shape was natural — from a crystal that looked like an enormous yellow diamond.

Leticia's aching body froze into a stillness so deep she thought she might never move again. Her breathing slowed; her hungry lungs grew so tight she could hardly breathe, even though her heart was racing and sweat, sharp and cold, oozed from her skin, soaking her clothes, stiffening her already bruised muscles.

She couldn't take her eyes off the massive crystal, its warm golden luminescence flashing like a lighthouse, imprinting its image into her madly racing brain. She'd seen photos of the recently discovered Golden Jubilee, a massive octahedral yellow-brown diamond weighing more than one hundred and fifty grams, found in Kimberley's prolific blue ground.

This one — this unearthly beauty — looked twice its size.

The paralysis holding her loosened its grip, and she sucked in air, a crazed laugh forcing its way past her throat.

'Am I bosbefok?' she asked the walls. 'Am I crazy, or is that a diamond?'

When no answer came from the painted figures, she said, 'Only one way to find out!'

Lying flat on her stomach until the gleaming stone aligned with her face, she stretched forward to grasp it. Her hands trembled so much that she moved slowly, cradling the precious stone, wet and slippery, with the tight grip of a mother holding a newborn baby, wriggling backwards until she was far enough away from the pool to sit with her back against the rock wall and examine her find.

There was enough light from the cave's entrance for her to see that the raw diamond was a vivid canary yellow, without even a hint of orange or brown to mar its clarity. The pure, intense yellow was translucent, its perfect octahedral shape marginally distorted by trigons etched onto two faces.

As she twisted it this way and that to catch the faint light, the flat, lustrous faces looked as if they'd been polished, but that was impossible. No miner would have left this gem behind when the old town died; no gem cutter from a world without the technological advancements of the late twentieth century could have shaped the raw perfection of this natural stone.

Leticia clutched it to her chest, laughing and — she who never cried —crying. 'Who needs a lucky quartz,' she asked, 'when I've got this! The company will give me millions as a finder's bonus. And I'll be famous! They can call it the Calder Yellow!' As her excitement rose, her fingers flexed and curled around the diamond, her heart burning with a passion never felt before.

She heard a voice then, a rustle lifting the hairs on her arms, skittering her pulse into an erratic pounding.

'Who's there?' she hissed, eyes darting around the cave.

The shadows in the cave lengthened, the painted figures on the wall sliding off the walls as the light dimmed. Clasping the diamond tightly into her chest, hunching over to protect it, Leticia scrambled sideways, closer to the cave's mouth, wincing as her bruised body scraped against the volcanic rock, her breath rasping as dread clutched her chest.

It's only the wind, she told herself as the elongated shadows glided towards her. *Or a thirsty animal. The hauntings are just a legend.*

When life threw challenges at her, she wasn't a woman who cried, and she wasn't a woman who screeched. But, as long hands clawed her clothes, Leticia screamed and screamed, the same faces she'd hallucinated during her fall into the gully surrounding her, their mournful voices wailing above a howling wind that had arisen, crowding her, jostling her, trying to steal her diamond.

'*I* found it!' she yelled, whipping from side to side, struggling to break free from the insistent hands while clinging to the diamond. 'Go away! It's *mine!*'

As she spoke, an unholy cry of pain surrounded her, filling the air with palpable grief, a loss so heavy the air groaned. Under the weight of it, she fell to her knees, hunching over and whimpering as the diamond rolled into the sand. She let it go, covering her ears and closing her eyes to block out the churning horror surrounding her.

The shrieking wind stopped as quickly as it had arisen.

Leticia stayed motionless until her muscles ached with numbness. The silence had become infinite, and the heat seared her bare head. Her eyelids fluttered open, and she squinted in the fiery sunshine. Dropping her hands onto her thighs, she looked at the angle of shade thrown by the old houses, then at the length of the shadows in the cave behind her, before checking her wristwatch, its black and green face scratched but miraculously intact after her fall.

It's not even midday, Leticia thought, shaking her head and hooking the damp tendrils of hair behind her ears. Less than twelve hours of her life had passed since the clattering roof had woken her in the early hours. And yet she felt as exhausted and battered as if she'd lived through a year of hard labour, as if something inside her, some dangerous flaw she'd previously been unaware of, had tested her to her limits, and she'd escaped a terrible fate by the smallest of margins. Now she knew what her flaw was, and, like a flawed diamond in the hands of a master gem cutter, she could polish the flaw out of her soul.

There was no time for Leticia to explore the old ghost town. She had to climb out of the gully to find her way back to the vein of black rock, where she'd abandoned her backpack and supplies.

Ignoring the flare of pain in her muscles, Leticia pushed herself upright. Her jaw clenched, and she began the slow trudge up the side of the gully. Eventually, she dragged herself back over the top, and as she glanced back for one last look at the ghost town, she gasped, a hand splaying over her chest to stop her heart from leaping out.

The town had disappeared. There was nothing in the gully except sand and a few scattered boulders; one cleaved open by an enormous !kharos plant growing from the fissure, its two leaves splaying over the ground in wild abandon. Leticia knew these strange plants could live for over a thousand years; this one looked like it had survived two thousand years of struggle and still thrived. No matter what obstacles she faced, even if she never found a colossal diamond to win her international fame and fortune, she had come to love this life in this quiet desert paradise where the wind talked to those who listened. She, too, would survive and flourish.

Cleophas was waiting at the quarry gate as she crossed Orion's Pass. 'Did the hunt go well, Letty?' he asked, a slight tic clenching his jaw, a tension in his shoulders making him appear less easy-going than usual.

On the long trudge home, Leticia had thought about what would happen once she reported the vein of black rock with its multitude of crystal riches. None were as matchless as her yellow diamond, but each was uniquely beautiful. Still, the bulldozers, the mobile crushing plants, and the cranes would arrive, indiscriminately grinding everything— scorpions, tiny geckos, even the ancient !kharos plants — in their gaping jaws.

'There was nothing to hunt, Cleophas,' she said carefully. 'There was only the wind talking so much I got lost. How will I live that down tonight at The Desert Rose?'

A slow smile crossed Cleophas' face, deepening the wrinkles already forming at the sides of his eyes.

'Ah, Letty,' he said, bowing his head. 'You were never lost. You were only following your dream.'

Taking her backpack from her aching shoulders, without saying a word about the wetness filming her eyes, he nodded toward the compound. 'Come, Letty, it's time to go home. You deserve a long, cool vodka.'

Leticia knew as well as Cleophas did that before she'd entered The Desert Rose for the first time, he'd agreed to her request that her special bottle of vodka be filled with only water.

'Let's go home, Cleophas,' she said. 'You can pour me a double.'

As her laughter chased away her tears, the wind sighed and settled into the coming night with barely a whisper, for it knew, as it knew everything, that a new dawn was coming.

About the Author

J A Croome lives in Johannesburg, the economic powerhouse of Africa, but her childhood playground was the Zimbabwean bush. With the beat of Africa in her blood, her writing is set in this continent, which has deep passion as its heart.

The driving motivation of her writing is the search for love in all its forms. Judy Ann writes because she believes words have great power: they can bring comfort and hope. They can reveal secrets and lies. And, while they may not change the world, they can—at their best—change people's lives, even if only for a moment.

Judy Ann was married to the late Dr. Beric Croome. She loves cats and enjoys reading, writing, nature, old churches with their ancient graveyards, exploring the ancient arts of tarot and astrology, meditation, and silence.

Acknowledgements

Writing the short stories in THE SAND PEOPLE was both challenging and rewarding. Between nearly two years of major eye surgery, crushing self-doubt about my writing, and learning to live without my beloved Beric, reaching for every word was a struggle I couldn't have won without the generous support of several key people.

At nearly ninety years old, my mother, Dawn Heinemann, took over all practical housekeeping duties when I disappeared into my cave to wrestle with my writing demons. Her fierce spirit of independence gave me the gift of freedom to write, while the example she set and her unconditional mother's love gave me the inner strength to complete this book.

My family and all my friends (old and new) enrich my life enormously, as does that cat extraordinaire, Mighty Mr Mittens, the sweetest, bravest familiar any writer can ask for.

I am incredibly grateful for the presence of Dr Joanne Pautz, Jess van Herwijnen, Chris Hajec, and Gary Chapman in my life. Joanne's unfaltering friendship and support; Chris's acceptance and understanding; Jess's uncanny ability and willingness to provide wise guidance whenever needed; and the lengthy debates with Gary on everything from philosophy to fishing make me happy and emphasise the importance of human connection in the necessarily introverted life of a writer.

No acknowledgement is complete without honouring my ancestors and loved ones in spirit, in particular, my late father, Isaac Benjamin Heinemann, a gifted clairvoyant and dowser, and my late husband, Dr Beric Croome, whose brilliant intellect and deep spirituality made him unique. Always remembered, always at my side.

My cherished writing friends for over twenty years, Leonie Anderson, Janet Chamberlain, Debs Valentyne, and Liesel van Wyk, have, once again, improved my work with their editing skills and insightful comments.

While the creative expression of all stories in this anthology is mine, I must thank my brother-in-law Ian Cockerill for his technical advice in "Where the Wind Talks." Any error of fact is due to my creative interpretation of his extensive mining knowledge.

I am also grateful to Wendy Bow of Apple Pie Graphics for the beautiful cover design and Dave Henderson of My eBook (South Africa) for his technical expertise.

Judy Ann Croome (2024)

Other Publications
(as Judy Croome)

Non-Fiction

Street Smart Taxpayers: A Practical Guide to Your Rights in South Africa (Juta Law, 2017 – co-authored with Dr. Beric Croome)

Poetry

the dust of hope: rune poems (Aztar Press, 2021)
drop by drop: poems of loss (Aztar Press, 2020)
a stranger in a strange land (Aztar Press, 2015)
a Lamp at Midday (Aztar Press, 2012)

Fiction

The Weight of a Feather and Other Stories (Aztar Press, 2013).
Dancing in the Shadows of Love (3rd Edition, Aztar Press, 2018)

Connect Online

Web: www.judycroome.com
Instagram: judy_croome
YouTube: Judy Croome
GoodReads   Judy Croome

the dust of hopes (rune poems)
by Judy Croome

Reviews from readers around the globe

'This was such an intriguing and captivating book of poetry. The idea that each author's poems represented an individual rune was unique. The balance the author struck between the representation of the ancient runes and the modern-day struggles we all face internally and externally was perfectly captured. Heartfelt, beautifully written, and thoughtful in its approach, *the dust of hope: rune poems* is a must-read book of poetry. A calming and intuitive experience, and a wonderful read overall.' ~ Anthony

'*the dust of hope* is a beautiful collection of poems inspired by the runes of the Elder Futhark. This collection is both thought-provoking and soul-stirring. Does it call us out? Yes, but humanity needs to hear it. Highly recommended.' ~ Michelle

'*the dust of hope – rune poems* by Judy Croome is such an interesting take on both poems and runes. With the uniqueness of the poems, I found myself flying through this one, completely enraptured from start to finish.' ~ Star

'A wonderful collection of poems that I would definitely read over and over.' ~ Wendy

Drop by Drop (poems of loss)
by Judy Croome

Letters from readers around the globe

'Tender, heartfelt and uplifting. I loved these poems.'

'A stunning anthology of poetry. The emotion is raw without being hysterical, and the English is beautiful – a consistently powerful use of the language without formulas, rules, and conventionality. It reads "brightly" - like burnished silver.'

'A thought-provoking and vivid reflection of what anyone nursing a terminally ill loved one goes through. Full of emotional depth and the thoughts people must be feeling but can't express, these poems are of great comfort - reading them will make people feel less alone.'

'This volume cuts to the heart of the up-and-down moments of walking the path with a terminally ill loved one. Croome managed to voice feelings for which I could not find words. Her poems paint pictures of large and small moments in the journey of grief. This volume will be a wonderful companion for people on the same journey: your feelings are valid, and you are not alone - there is hope and strength to be found in this part of life, too.'

a stranger in a strange land
by Judy Croome

Reviews from readers around the globe

'Often deceptively simple phrasing makes *a stranger in a strange land* a very accessible, honest, open and earnest collection. Though many of the poems have grim themes, a redeeming sense of hope underpins the book, along with the sense that Croome still adheres to her simple core values despite disappointments, sorrow and despair along the way. And chief of all of these is summed up in just one word: love. A roller-coaster of a collection that will inspire readers to ride out the ups and downs of their own lives, and to always find balance and hope by considering the bigger picture.' — Vine Leaves Literary Journal.

'These poems are vivid and absorbing and deliver a punch that will make you see, make you feel, make you understand even when you don't want to, but there's a good balance, enough to soothe your soul along the way.'

'*a stranger in a strange land* shows Croome exploring what it is to be human. The poet's heartfelt humanity and humility are shown, but it is in her lyric poems that she is more effective, using form to capture the tension between mind and heart.'

'Some poems are a joyful celebration of life; others a harrowing dissection of the soul. Each poem in *a stranger in a strange land* is a unique and sparkling gem in its own right, and as a whole, this volume makes for a riveting reading experience.'

The Weight of a Feather
by Judy Croome

*Reviews of this collection of short stories from
readers around the globe*

'Croome is an artist whose canvas is the blank
page and whose medium is words. She paints
pictures. Some sparse, some detailed. Some
modernistic, some classical. But each can be re-read
many times over.'

'A beautiful set of stories that has something very
few short story collections have — variety. Just like
the land Croome comes from, the complexity of this
collection offers a little something for everyone.'

'A wonderful collection that I'll be reading over
and over again.'

'These are some of the best short stories I've ever
read. Some of them are no more than a page and a
half, but every one of them packs a wallop! The best
part of these stories is how Croome has taken men
and women from all walks of life, all ages, and from
all kinds of locations and made them relatable.'

a Lamp at Midday
by Judy Croome

Reviews from readers around the globe

'Croome's poems are never too bleak or her voice too bitter; her warmth and love are always with you. A must-read!'

'Croome's writing feels tranquillising, as her poems reach their impact through their inherent quietness.'

'A collection of beautifully written poems.'

'The poems are evocative, sincere and heartfelt and stirred up many emotions for me. There is intellectual enjoyment, too.'

'The first half of *a Lamp at Midday* is a brave and haunting love letter to Croome's father, while the second half focuses on a different kind of love and rebirth.'

Dancing in the Shadows of Love
by Judy Croome

*Reviews of this magical realism novel from readers
around the globe*

'Although set in contemporary South Africa,
magical realism frees the story somewhat to explore
complex spiritual themes. For a first novel, *Dancing
in the Shadows of Love* is very well written, with
nuanced character development and solid plotting.'

'Full of brutal honesty, the story is not easy to
read. About facing fears and bigotries and coming to
terms with the opinions of those who refuse to
honestly look inside themselves for the truth, it's also
a story of hope and coming to terms with what could
be perceived as one's own differences from the norm
of mainstream society.'

'Gorgeous, brilliant, heart-breaking, uplifting,
empowering ... and more! Although *Dancing in the
Shadows of Love* takes place in a purposely undefined
place and time, the characters are painfully real. The
story follows three women, each with a damaged soul,
as they yearn to be loved, but first, they need to define
love and to do that, they must learn to forgive. The
mysterious Enoch is their guide for this spiritual
journey. Croome's writing is impeccable, and her
insight into the soul of man astounding.'

Printed in Great Britain
by Amazon